HERE COMES TROUBLE
Debbie Macomber

Harlequin Books

TORONTO • NEW YORK • LONDON
AMSTERDAM • PARIS • SYDNEY • HAMBURG
STOCKHOLM • ATHENS • TOKYO • MILAN

ISBN 0-373-03148-3

Harlequin Romance first edition September 1991

HERE COMES TROUBLE

"I'm quitting the paper!"

"What? Why?" Kramer lowered himself slowly to the sofa. "You're overreacting, Maryanne! There's no need to do anything that drastic."

"There's every need. You said so yourself. What you wrote is true—if I'm half as good a reporter as I think I am, I would've got this job without my father's help."

"That's no reason for quitting *The Review!*" he shouted, rushing to his feet.

"Nothing you say is going to change my mind," Maryanne informed him primly. "The time has come to cut myself loose and to sink or swim on my own."

"Listen to me, would you?" Kramer's handsome face was pained. "You're leaping into the deep end, you don't know how to swim—and the lifeguard's off duty!"

Debbie Macomber is an American writer born in the state of Washington, where she still lives. She and her electrician husband have four children, all of them teenagers. They also support a menagerie that includes horses, cats, a dog and some guinea pigs. Debbie's successful writing career actually started in childhood, when her brother copied—and sold—her diary! She's gone on to a considerably wider readership since then, as a prolific and popular author published in several different romance lines. She says she wrote her first book because she fell in love with Harlequin Romance novels—and wanted to write her own.

Books by Debbie Macomber

CHAPTER ONE

"MARYANNE SIMPSON of the New York Simpsons, I presume?"

Maryanne glared at the man standing across the room from her in the reception area of the radio station. She pointedly ignored his sarcasm, keeping her baby-blue eyes as emotionless as possible.

Kramer Adams—Seattle's most popular journalist—looked nothing like the polished professional man in the black-and-white photo that headed his daily column. Instead he resembled a well-known disheveled television detective. He even wore a wrinkled raincoat, one that looked as if he'd slept in it for an entire week.

"Or should I call you Deb?" he taunted.

"Ms. Simpson will suffice," she said in her best finishing-school voice. The rival newspaperman was cocky and arrogant and the best damn journalist Maryanne had ever read. Maryanne was a good columnist herself, or at least she was desperately striving to become one. Her father, who owned the *Seattle Review* and twelve other daily newspapers nationwide, had seen to it that she was given this once-in-a-lifetime opportunity with the Seattle paper. She was working hard to prove herself. Perhaps too hard. That was when the trouble had begun.

"So how's the heart?" Kramer asked, reaching for a magazine and idly flipping through the dog-eared pages. "Is it still bleeding with all those liberal views of yours?"

Maryanne ignored the question, removed her navy blue wool coat and neatly folded it over the back of a chair. "My heart is just fine, thank you."

With a sound she could only describe as a snicker, he threw himself down on the padded chair and indolently brought an ankle up to rest on his knee.

Maryanne sat across from him, stiff and straight in the high-backed chair, and boldly met his eyes. Everything she needed to know about Kramer Adams could be seen in his face. The strong well-defined lines of his jaw told her how stubborn he could be. His eyes were dark, intelligent and intense. And his mouth, well, that was another story altogether. It seemed to wrestle with itself before ever breaking into a smile, as if a gesture of amusement went against his very nature. Kramer wasn't smiling now. And Maryanne wasn't about to let him know how much he intimidated her. Some emotion must have shone in her eyes, because he said abruptly, "You're the one who started this, you know?"

Maryanne was well aware of that. But this rivalry between them had begun unintentionally, at least on her part. The very day that the morning edition of the competition, the *Seattle Sun,* published Kramer's column on solutions to the city's housing problem, the *Review* had run Maryanne's piece on the same subject. Kramer's article was meant to be satirical while Maryanne's was deadly serious. Her mistake was in stating that there were those in the city who apparently found the situation amusing, and she blasted anyone who behaved so irresponsibly. This was not a joking matter, she'd pointed out.

It was as if she'd read Kramer's column and set out to reprimand him personally for his cavalier attitude before the entire western half of Washington state.

Two days later, Kramer's column poked fun at her, asking what Ms. High Society could possibly know about affordable housing. Clearly a debutante had never had to worry about the roof over her head, he'd snarled. But more than that, he'd made her suggestions to alleviate the growing problem sound both frivolous and impractical.

Her next column came out the same evening and referred to tough pessimistic reporters who took themselves much too seriously. She went so far as to make fun of a fictional Seattle newsman who resembled Kramer Adams to a T.

Kramer retaliated once more, and Maryanne seethed. Obviously she'd have to be the one to put an end to this silliness. She hoped that not responding to Kramer's latest attack would terminate their rivalry, but she should have known better. An hour after her column on community spirit had hit the newsstands, KJBR, a local radio station, called, requesting Maryanne to give a guest editorial. She'd immediately agreed, excited and honored at the invitation. It wasn't until later that she learned Kramer Adams would also be speaking. The format was actually a celebrity debate, a fact of which she'd been blithely unaware.

The door opened and a tall dark-haired woman walked into the station's reception area. "I'm Liz Walters," she said, two steps into the room. "I produce the news show. I take it you two know each other?"

"Like family," Kramer muttered with that cocky grin of his.

"We introduced ourselves no more than five minutes ago," Maryanne rebutted stiffly.

"Good," Liz said without glancing up from her clipboard. "If you'll both come this way, we'll get you set up in the control booth."

From her brief conversation with the show's host, Brian Campbell, Maryanne learned that the show taped Thursday night wouldn't air until Sunday evening.

When they were both seated inside the control booth, Maryanne withdrew two typed pages from her purse. Not to be outdone, Kramer made a show of pulling a small notepad from the huge pocket of his crumpled raincoat.

Brian Campbell began the show with a brief introduction, presenting the evening's subject: the growing popularity of the Seattle area. He then turned the microphone over to Maryanne, who was to speak first.

Forcing herself to relax, she took a deep calming breath, tucked her long auburn hair behind her ears and started speaking. She managed to keep her voice low and as well modulated as her nerves would allow.

"The word's out," she said, glancing quickly at her notes. "Seattle has been rated one of top cities in the country for several years running. Is it any wonder Californians are moving up in droves, attracted by the increasing economic growth, the lure of pure fresh air and beautiful clean waters? Seattle has appeal, personality and class."

As she warmed to her subject, her voice gained confidence and conviction. She'd fallen in love with Seattle when she'd visited for a two-day layover before flying to Hawaii. The trip had been a college graduation gift from her parents. She'd returned to New York one week later full of enthusiasm, not for the tourist-cluttered islands, but for the brief glimpse she'd had of the Emerald City.

From the first, she'd intended to return to the Pacific Northwest. Instead she'd taken a job as a nonfiction editor in one of her father's New York publishing houses; she'd been so busy that traveling time was limited. That editorial job lasted almost eighteen months, and although Maryanne thoroughly enjoyed it, she longed to write herself, and put her journalism skills to work.

Samuel Simpson must have sensed her restlessness because he mentioned an opening at the *Seattle Review,* a long-established paper, when they met in Nantucket over Labor Day weekend. Maryanne had plied him with questions, mentioning more than once how she'd fallen in love with Seattle. Her father had grinned, chewing vigorously on the end of his cigar, and looked toward his wife of twenty-seven years before he'd casually reached for the telephone. After a single call that lasted less than three minutes, Samuel announced the job was hers. Within two weeks, Maryanne was packed and on her way west.

"In conclusion I'd like to remind our audience that there's no turning back now," Maryanne said. "Seattle sits as a polished jewel in the beautiful Pacific Northwest. Seattle, the Emerald City, awaits even greater prosperity, even more progress."

She set her papers aside and smiled in the direction of the host, relieved to be finished. She watched in dismay as Kramer scowled at her, then slipped his notepad back inside his pocket. He apparently planned to wing it.

Kramer—who needed, Brian declared, no introduction—leaned toward the microphone. He glanced at

Maryanne, frowned once more, and slowly shook his head.

"Give me a break, Ms. Simpson!" he cried. "Doesn't anyone realize it rains here? Did you know that until recently, if Seattle went an entire week without rain, we sacrificed a virgin? Unfortunately we were running low on those until you moved into town."

Maryanne barely managed to restrain a gasp.

"Why do you think Seattle has remained so beautiful?" Kramer continued. "Why do you think we aren't suffering from the pollution problems so prevalent in Southern California and elsewhere? You seem to believe Seattle should throw open her arms and invite the world to park on our unspoiled doorstep. My advice to you, and others like you, is to go back where you came from. We don't want you turning Seattle into another L.A.—or New York."

The hair on the back of Maryanne's neck bristled. Although he spoke in general terms, his words seemed to be directed solely at her. He was telling her, in effect, to pack up her suitcase and head home to Mommy and Daddy where she belonged.

When Kramer finished, they were each given two minutes for a rebuttal.

"Some of what you have to say is true," Maryanne admitted through clenched teeth. "But you can't turn back progress. Only a fool," she said pointedly, "would try to keep families from settling in Washington state. You can argue until you've lost your voice, but it isn't going to help. The population in this area is going to explode in the next few years whether you approve or not."

"That's probably true, but it doesn't mean I have to sit still and let it happen. In fact, I intend to do everything I can to put a stop to it. We in Seattle have a way of life to protect and a duty to future generations. If growth continues in this vein, our schools will soon be overcrowded, our homes so overpriced that no one except those from out of state will be able to afford housing—and that's only if they can find it. If that's what you want, then fine, bask in your ignorance."

"What do you suggest?" Maryanne burst out. "Setting up road blocks?"

"That's a start," Kramer returned sarcastically. "Something's got to be done before this area becomes another urban disaster."

Maryanne rolled her eyes. "Do you honestly think you're going to single-handedly turn back the tide of progress?"

"I'm sure as hell going to try."

"That's ridiculous."

"And that's our Celebrity Debate for this evening," Brian Campbell said quickly, cutting off any further argument. "Join us next week when our guests will be City Council candidates Nick Fraser and Robert Hall."

The microphone was abruptly switched off. "That was excellent," the host said, flashing them a wide enthusiastic smile. "Thank you both."

"You've got your head buried in the sand," Maryanne felt obliged to inform Kramer, although she knew it wouldn't do any good. She dropped her notes back in her purse and snapped it firmly shut, as if to say the subject was now closed.

"You may be right," Kramer said with a grin. "But at least the sand is on a pollution-free beach. If you have your way, it'll soon be cluttered with—"

"I have my way?" she cried. "You make it sound as though I'm solely responsible for the Puget Sound growth rate."

"You are responsible, and those like you."

"Well, excuse me," she muttered sarcastically. She nodded politely to Brian Campbell, then headed back to the reception room where she'd left her coat. To her annoyance Kramer followed her, grumbling every step of the way.

"I don't excuse you, Deb."

"I asked you to use my name," she said furiously, "and it isn't Deb."

Crossing his arms over his chest, Kramer leaned lazily against the doorjamb while she retrieved her wool coat.

Maryanne crammed her arms into the sleeves and nearly tore off the buttons in her rush to leave. The way he stood there studying her did little to cool her temper.

"And another thing . . ." she muttered.

"You mean there's more?"

"You're darn right there is. That crack about virgins was intolerably rude! I . . . I expected better of you."

"Hell, it's true."

"How would you know?"

He grinned that insufferable grin of his, infuriating her even more.

"Don't you have anything better to do than follow me around?" she demanded, stalking out of the room.

"Not particularly. Fact is, I've been looking forward to meeting you."

Once she'd recovered from the shock of learning that he'd be her opponent in this radio debate, Maryanne had eagerly anticipated this evening, too. Long before she'd arrived at the radio station, she'd planned to tell Kramer how much she admired his work. This silly rivalry between them was exactly that: silly. She hadn't meant to step on his toes and would have willingly called and cleared the air if he hadn't attacked her in print at the earliest opportunity.

"Sure you wanted to meet me. Hurling insults to my face must be far more fun."

He laughed at that and Maryanne was amazed at how rich and friendly his amusement sounded.

"Come on, Simpson, don't take everything so personally. Admit it. We've been having a good time poking fun at each other."

Maryanne didn't say anything for several moments. Actually he was partially right. She *had* enjoyed their exchanges, although she wouldn't have admitted that earlier. She wasn't entirely sure she wanted to now.

"Admit it," he coaxed, again with a grin.

That uneven smile of his was her undoing. "It hasn't exactly been *fun,*" she answered reluctantly, "but it has been . . . interesting."

"That's what I thought." He thrust his hands into his pockets, looking pleased with himself.

She glanced at him appraisingly. The man's appeal was definitely of the rugged variety: his outrageous charm—Maryanne wasn't sure charm was really the right word—his craggy face and solid compact build. She'd been surprised to discover he wasn't as tall as she'd imagined. In fact, he was probably less than six feet.

"Word has it Daddy was the one responsible for landing you this cushy job," he commented, disrupting her assessment.

"Cushy?" she cried, infuriated. "You've got to be kidding!" She often put in twelve-hour days slaving over her computer, trying to come up with a column that was both relevant and entertaining. In the four weeks since she'd joined the *Seattle Review* staff, she'd worked damn hard. She had something to prove to herself, not only to herself but to her peers.

"So being a journalist isn't everything it's cracked up to be?"

"I didn't say that," she returned heatedly. To be perfectly honest, Maryanne had never tried harder at anything. Her pride and a whole lot more was riding on the outcome of the next few months. Samuel Simpson's daughter or not, she was on probation, after which her performance would be reviewed by the managing editor.

"I wonder if you've ever done anything without Daddy's approval."

"I wonder if you've always been this rude."

He chuckled at that. "Almost always. Like I said, don't take it personally."

With her leather purse securely tucked under her arm, she headed for the exit, which Kramer was effectively blocking. "Excuse me, please."

"Always so polite," he murmured before he straightened, allowing her to pass.

Kramer followed her to the elevator, annoying her even more. Maryanne felt his scrutiny, and it flustered her. She knew she was reasonably attractive, but she also knew that no one was going to rush forward with a banner and a tiara. Her mouth was just a little too full, her eyes a little too round. Her hair had been fire-engine red the entire time she was growing up, but it had darkened to a deep auburn in her early twenties, a fact for which she remained truly grateful. Maryanne had always hated her red hair and the wealth of freckles that accompanied it. No one else in her family had been cursed with red hair, not to mention freckles. Her mother's hair was a beautiful blond and her father's a rich chestnut. Even her younger brothers had escaped her fate. If it weren't for the distinctive high Simpson forehead and deep blue eyes, Maryanne might have suspected she'd been adopted. But that wasn't the case. Instead she'd been forced to discover early in life how unfair heredity could be.

The elevator arrived, and both Maryanne and Kramer stepped inside. Kramer leaned against the side—he always seemed to be leaning, Maryanne noticed. Leaning and staring. He was studying her again; she could feel his eyes as profoundly as a caress.

"Would you kindly stop," she snapped.

"What?"

"Staring at me!"

"I'm curious."

"About what?" She was curious about him, too, but far too civilized to make an issue of it the way he was doing.

"I just wanted to see if all that blue blood showed."

"Oh, honestly!"

"I am being honest," he answered. "You know, you intrigue me, Simpson. Have you eaten?"

Maryanne's heart immediately raced with excitement at the offhand question. He seemed to be leading up to suggesting they dine together. Unfortunately she'd been around Kramer long enough to realize she couldn't trust the man. Anything she said or did would more than likely show up in that column of his.

"I've got an Irish stew simmering in a pot at home," she murmured, dismissing the invitation before he could offer it.

"Great! I love stew."

Maryanne opened her mouth to tell him she had no intention of asking him into her home. Not after the things he'd said about her in his column. But when she turned to tell him so, their eyes met. Brown eyes clashed with blue ones. His were deep and dark and almost...she couldn't be sure, but she thought she saw a faint glimmer of admiration. The edge of his mouth quirked upward with an unmistakable hint of challenge. He looked as if he expected her to reject him.

Against her better judgment, and knowing she'd live to regret this, Maryanne found herself smiling.

"My apartment's on Spring Street," she murmured.

"Good. I'll follow you."

She lowered her gaze, feeling chagrined and already a little regretful about the whole thing. "I didn't drive."

"Is your chauffeur waiting?" he asked, his voice and eyes mocking her in a manner that was practically friendly.

"I took a cab," she said, glancing away from him. "It's a way of life in Manhattan and I'm not accustomed to dealing with a car. So I don't have one." She half expected him to make some derogatory comment and was thankful when he didn't.

"I'll give you a lift then."

He'd parked his car, a surprisingly stylish sedan, in a lot close to the waterfront. The late-September air was brisk, and Maryanne braced herself against it as Kramer cleared the litter off the passenger seat for her.

She slipped inside, grateful to be out of the chill. It didn't take her more than a couple of seconds to realize that Kramer treated his car the same way he treated his raincoat. The front and the back seat of the sedan were both cluttered with empty paper cups, old newspapers and several paperback novels. Mysteries, she noted. The great Kramer Adams read mysteries. A container filled with loose change was propped inside his ashtray.

While Maryanne searched for the seat belt, Kramer raced around the front of the car, slid inside and quickly started the engine. "I hope there's a place to park off Spring."

"Oh, don't worry," Maryanne quickly assured him, "I've got valet service."

Kramer murmured something under his breath. Had she made an effort, she might have been able to hear, but she figured she was probably better off not knowing.

He turned up the heater and Maryanne was warmed by a blast of air. "Let me know if that gets too hot for you."

"Thanks, I'm fine."

"Hot" seemed to describe their relationship. From the first, Maryanne had inadvertently got herself into scalding water with Kramer, water that came closer to boiling point each time a new column appeared. "Hot" also described the way they seemed to ignite sparks off each other. The radio show had proved that much.

Nevertheless, Maryanne was grateful for the opportunity to bridge their differences, because despite everything, she genuinely admired Kramer's writing.

They chatted amicably enough until Kramer pulled into the crescent-shaped driveway of The Seattle, the luxury apartment complex where she lived.

Max, the doorman, opened her car door, his stoic face breaking into a smile as he recognized her. When

Kramer climbed out of the driver's side, Maryanne watched as Max's smile slowly turned into a frown, as though he wasn't certain Kramer was appropriate company for a respectable young lady.

"Max, this is Mr. Adams from the *Seattle Sun.*"

"Kramer Adams?" Max's expression altered immediately. "I read your work faithfully, Mr. Adams. You gave ol' Larson hell last month. From what I heard, your column was what forced him to resign from City Council."

Kramer had given Maryanne hell, too, but she refrained from mentioning it. She doubted Max had ever read her work or was even aware that Kramer had been referring to her in his column earlier in the month.

"Would you see to Mr. Adam's car?" Maryanne asked.

"Right away, Ms. Simpson."

Burying his hands in his pockets, Kramer followed Maryanne into the extravagantly decorated foyer with its huge crystal chandelier and bubbling fountain. "My apartment's on the eleventh floor," she said, pushing the elevator button.

"Not the penthouse suite?" he teased.

Maryanne smiled weakly in response. While they rode upward, she concentrated on taking her keys from her purse to hide her sudden nervousness. Her heart was banging against her ribs. Now that Kramer was practically at her door, she wondered how she'd let this happen. After the things he'd called her, the least of which were Ms. High Society, Miss Debutante and Daddy's Darling, she felt more than a little vulnerable sharing his company.

"Are you ready to change your mind?" he asked, as though he'd read her thoughts.

"No, of course not." she lied.

She noticed—but sincerely hoped Kramer didn't— that her hand was shaking when she inserted the key.

She turned on the light as she walked into the spacious apartment. Kramer followed her, his brows raised at the sight of the modern white leather and chrome furniture. There was even a fireplace.

"Nice place you've got here," he said, glancing around.

She thought she detected sarcasm in his voice, then decided it was what she could expect from him all evening; she might as well get used to it.

"I'll take your raincoat," she said. Considering the fondness with which he wore the thing, he might well choose to eat in it, too.

To Maryanne's surprise, he handed it to her, then walked over to the fireplace and lifted a family photo from the mantel. The picture had been taken several summers earlier, when they'd all been sailing off Martha's Vineyard. Maryanne was looking into the wind and laughing at the antics of her younger brothers. It certainly wasn't her most flattering photo. In fact she looked as if she was gasping for air after being too long underwater. The wind had caught her red hair, its color even more pronounced against the backdrop of white sails.

"The two young men with me are my brothers. My mom and dad are at the helm."

Kramer stared at the picture for several seconds and then back at her. "So you're the only redhead."

"How kind of you to mention it."

"Hey, you're in luck. I happen to like redheads." He said this with such a lazy smile Maryanne couldn't possibly be offended.

"I'll check the stew," she said, after hanging up their coats. She hurried into the kitchen and lifted the lid of the pot. The pungent aroma of stewing lamb, vegetables and basil filled the apartment.

"You weren't kidding, were you?" Kramer asked, sounding mildly surprised.

"Kidding? About what?"

"The Irish stew."

"No. I put it on this morning, before I left for work. I've got one of those all-day cookers." After living on her own for the past couple of years, Maryanne had become a competent cook. When she'd rented her first apartment in New York, she used to stop off at a deli on her way home, but that had soon become monotonous. Over the course of several months, she'd discovered some excellent recipes for simple nutritious meals. Her father wasn't going to publish a cookbook by her perhaps, but she did manage to eat well.

"I thought the stew was an excuse not to have dinner with me," Kramer remarked conversationally. "I didn't know what to expect. You're my first deb."

"Some white wine?" she asked, ignoring his comment.

"Please."

Maryanne got a bottle from the refrigerator and expertly removed the cork. She filled them each a glass, then handed Kramer his and carried the bottle into the living room where she set it on the polished glass-topped coffee table. Sitting down on one end of the white leather sofa, she slipped off her shoes and tucked her feet beneath her.

Kramer sat at the other end, resting his ankle on his knee, making himself at home. "Dare I propose a toast?" he asked.

"Please."

"To Seattle," he said, his mischievous gaze meeting hers. "May she forever remain unspoiled." He reached over and touched the rim of her glass with his.

"To Seattle," Maryanne returned. "The most enchanting city on the West Coast."

"But, please, don't let anyone know," Kramer coaxed in a stage whisper.

"I'm not making any promises," she whispered back.

They tasted the wine, which had come highly recommended by a friend at the paper. Maryanne had only recently learned that wines from Washington state were quickly gaining a world reputation for excellence. Apparently the soil, a rich sandy loam over a volcanic base, was the key.

They talked about the wine for a few moments, and the conversation flowed naturally after that, as they compared experiences and shared impressions. Maryanne was surprised by how much she was enjoying the company of this man she'd considered a foe. Actually, they did have several things in common. Perhaps she was enjoying his company simply because she was lonely, but she didn't think that was entirely true. She'd been too busy with work to do any socializing; she occasionally saw a few people from the paper, but other than that, she hadn't had time to establish any friendships.

After a second glass of wine, feeling warm and relaxed, Maryanne was willing to admit exactly how isolated she'd felt since moving to Seattle.

"It's been so long since I went out on a real date."

"There does seem to be a shortage of Ivy League guys in Seattle."

She giggled and nodded. "At least Dad's not sending along a troupe of eligible men for me to meet. I enjoyed living in New York, don't get me wrong, but every time I turned around a man was introducing himself and telling me my father had given him my phone number. You're the first man I've had dinner with that Dad didn't handpick for me since I moved out on my own."

"I hate to tell you this, sugar, but I have the distinct impression your daddy would take one look at me and have me arrested."

"That's not the least bit true," Maryanne argued. "My dad isn't a snob, only... only if you do meet him take off the raincoat, okay?"

"The raincoat?"

"It looks like you sleep in it. All you need is a hat and a scrap of paper with Press scrawled on it sticking out of the band—you'd look like you worked for the *Planet* in Metropolis."

"I hate to disillusion you, sugar, but I'm not Ivy League and I'm not Superman."

"Oh, darn," she said, snapping her fingers. "And we had such an interesting thing going." She was feeling too mellow to remind him not to call her sugar.

"So how old are you?" Kramer wanted to know. "Twenty-one?"

"Three," she amended. "And you?"

"A hundred and three in comparison."

Maryanne wasn't entirely sure what he meant, but she let that pass, too. It felt good to have someone to talk to, someone who was her contemporary, or at least close to being her contemporary.

"If you don't want to tell me how old you are, then at least fill in some of the details of your life."

"Trust me, my life isn't nearly as interesting as yours."

"Bore me then."

"All right," he said, drawing a deep breath. "My family was dirt-poor. Dad disappeared about the time I was ten and Mom took on two jobs to make ends meet. Get the picture?"

"Yes." She hesitated. "What about women?"

"I've had a long and glorious history."

"I'm not kidding, Kramer."

"You think I was?"

"You're not married."

"Not to my knowledge."

"Why not?"

He shrugged as if it was of little consequence. "No time for it. I came close once, but her family didn't consider my writing career noble enough. Her father tried to fix me up with a job."

"What happened?"

"Nothing much. I told her I was going to work for the newspaper, and she claimed if I really loved her I'd accept her father's generous offer. It didn't take me long to decide. I guess she was right—I didn't love her."

He sounded nonchalant, as if the episode hadn't cost him a moment's regret, but just looking at him told Maryanne otherwise. Kramer had been deeply hurt. Every sarcastic irreverent word he wrote suggested it.

In retrospect, Maryanne mused one afternoon several days later, she'd thoroughly enjoyed her evening with Kramer. They'd eaten, and Kramer had raved about her Irish stew until she flushed at his praise. She'd made them cups of café au lait while Kramer built a fire. They'd sat in front of the fireplace and talked for hours. He'd told her more about his own large family, his seven brothers and sisters. How he'd worked his way through two years of college, but was forced to give up his education when he couldn't afford to continue. As it turned out, he'd been grateful because that decision had led to his first newspaper job. And, as they say, the rest was history.

"You certainly seem to be in a good mood," her co-worker, Carol Riverside, said as she strolled past Maryanne's desk later that same afternoon. Carol was short, with a pixielike face and friendly manner. Maryanne had liked her from the moment they'd met.

"I'm in a fabulous mood," Maryanne said, smiling. Kramer had promised to pay her back by taking her out to dinner. He hadn't set a definite date, but she half expected to hear from him that evening.

"In that case, I hate to be the bearer of bad tidings, but someone has to tell you, and I was appointed."

"Tell me? What?" Maryanne glanced around the huge open office and noted that several faces were staring in her direction, all wearing sympathetic looks. "What's going on?" she demanded.

Carol moved her arm out from behind her and Maryanne noticed that she was holding a copy of the rival newspaper's morning edition. "It's Kramer Adams's column," Carol said softly, her eyes wide and compassionate.

"W-what did he say this time?"

"Well, let's put it this way. He titled it, 'My Evening with the Debutante.'"

CHAPTER TWO

MARYANNE WAS much too furious to stand still. She stalked her living room like a caged panther, her mind spitting and churning. A slow painful death was too good for Kramer Adams.

Her phone rang and she went into the kitchen to answer it. She reached for it so fast and hard she nearly ripped it off the wall. Rarely did she allow herself to become this angry, but complicating her fury was a deep and aching sense of betrayal. "Yes," she said forcefully.

"This is Max," her doorman announced. "Mr. Adams is here. Shall I send him up?"

For an instant Maryanne was too stunned to speak. The man had nerve, she'd say that much for him. Raw courage, too, if he knew the state of mind she was in.

"Ms. Simpson?"

It took Maryanne only about a second to decide. "Send him up," she said with deceptive calm.

Arms hugging her waist, Maryanne continued pacing. She was going to tell this man in no uncertain terms what she thought of his duplicity, his trickery. He might have assumed from their evening together that she was a gentle, forgiving soul who would quietly overlook this treachery. Well, if that was his belief, Maryanne was looking forward to enlightening him.

Her doorbell chimed and she turned to glare at it with narrowed eyes. Wishing her heart would stop pounding, she gulped in a deep breath, then walked calmly across the living room and opened the door.

"Hello, Maryanne," Kramer said, his eyes immediately meeting hers.

She stood exactly where she was, imitating his tactic of leaning against the frame and blocking the threshold.

"May I come in?" he asked mildly.

"I haven't decided yet." He was wearing the raincoat again, which looked even more disreputable than before.

"I take it you read the article?" he murmured, one eyebrow raised.

"Read it?" she nearly shouted. "Of course I read it, and so, it seems, did everyone else in Seattle. Did you honestly think I'd be able to hold my head up after that? Or was that your intention—humiliating me and...and making me a laughingstock?" She stabbed her index finger repeatedly against his solid chest. "And if you think no one'll figure out it was me just because you didn't use my name, think again."

"I take it you're angry?" He raised his eyebrows again, as if to suggest she was overreacting.

"Angry! Angry? That isn't the half of it, buster!" The problem with being raised in a God-fearing, flag-loving family was that the worst thing she could think of to call him out loud was *buster*. Plenty of other names flashed through her mind, but none she dared to verbalize. No doubt Kramer would delight in revealing this in his column, too.

Furious, she grabbed his tie and jerked him into the apartment. "You can come inside," she said.

"Thanks. I think I will," Kramer said wryly. He smoothed his tie, which drew her attention to the hard defined muscles of his chest. The last thing Maryanne wanted to do was notice how virile he looked, and she forced her gaze away from him.

Because it was impossible to stand still, she resumed her pacing. With the first rush of anger spent, she had no idea what to say to him, how to make him realize the enormity of what he'd done. Abruptly, she paused at the edge of her living room and pointed an accusing finger at him. "You have your nerve."

"What I said was true," Kramer stated, boldly meeting her glare. "If you'd bothered to read the article all the way through, objectively, you'd have noticed there were several complimentary statements."

"'An idealist, an optimist…'" she said, quoting what she remembered, the parts that had offended her the most. "You made me sound like Mary Poppins!"

"Surprisingly unspoiled and gentle," Kramer returned, "and very much a lady."

"You told the entire city I was lonely," she cried, mortified even to repeat the words.

"I didn't say you were lonely," Kramer insisted, sounding all too reasonable and controlled. That infuriated her even more. "I said you were away from your family for the first time."

She poked his chest again as she punctuated her speech. "But you made it sound like I should be in a day-care center!"

"I didn't imply anything of the kind," he contended. "And I did mention what a good cook you are."

"I'm supposed to be grateful for that? As I recall you said, I was 'surprisingly adept in the kitchen'—as if you were amazed I knew the difference between a goldfish bowl and an oven.''

''You're blowing the whole thing out of proportion.''

Maryanne barely heard him. ''The comment about my being insecure was the worst. You want security, buster, you're looking at security. My feet could be molded in cement, I'm that secure.'' Defiant angry eyes flashed to him as she pointed at her shoes.

Kramer didn't so much as blink. ''You work twice as hard as anyone else at the *Review,* and twice as many hours. You push yourself because you've got something to prove.''

A strained silence followed his words. Everything he said was true. She *did* work hard, she *was* trying to prove herself, and Kramer knew it. Except in high school and college, she'd had no experience working for a newspaper.

''Did you wake up one morning and decide to play Sigmund Freud with my life?'' she cried. ''Who, may I ask, gave you that right?''

''What I said is true, Maryanne. I don't expect you to admit it to me, but if you're honest, you'll at least admit it to yourself. Your family is your greatest asset and your weakest link. From everything I've read about the Simpsons, they're good people, but they've cheated you out of something important.''

''Exactly what do you mean by that?'' she snapped, ready to defend her father to the death, if need be. How dare this pompous, arrogant, argumentative man insult her family!

''You'll never know if you're a good enough journalist to get a job like this without your father's help.

He handed you this plum position and at the same time cheated you out of a just reward.''

Maryanne opened her mouth, an argument hot on the tip of her tongue. Instead, she lowered her gaze, realizing there was nothing she could say to defend herself. From the moment she arrived at the *Seattle Review,* she'd known that Carol Riverside was the one who'd earned the right to be the local-affairs columnist, not her. And yet Carol had been wonderfully supportive and kind.

"It wasn't my intention to insult you or your family," Kramer continued.

"Then why did you write that column?" she demanded, her voice heaving. "Did you honestly think I was going to be flattered by it?"

He'd been so quick with the answers that his silence caught her attention more effectively than anything he could have said. She watched as he started pacing. He drew his fingers roughly through his hair and his shoulders rose in a distinct sigh.

"I'm not entirely sure. In retrospect, I believe I wanted to set the record straight. At least that was my original intent. I realize I wrote more than I should have, but the piece was never meant to ridicule you. Whether you know it or not, you impressed the hell out of me the other night."

"Am I supposed to be grateful you chose to thank me publicly?"

"No," he answered sharply. Once more he jerked his fingers fiercely through his hair. He didn't wince, but Maryanne did—which was interesting, since only a few minutes earlier she'd been daydreaming about the joy she'd experience watching this man suffer.

"Inviting myself to dinner the other night was an impulse," he admitted grudgingly. "The words slipped out before I realized what I was saying. I don't know who was more surprised, you or me. I tried to act like I knew what I was doing, play it cool, that sort of thing. The fact is, I discovered I like you. Trust me, I wasn't in any frame of mind to talk civilly to you when you arrived at the radio station. All along I'd assumed you were a spoiled rich kid, but I was wrong. Since I'd published several pieces that suggested as much, I felt it was only fair to set the record straight. Besides, for a deb you aren't half-bad."

"Why is it every time you compliment me, I feel a knife between my shoulder blades?"

"We certainly don't have a whole lot in common," Kramer continued thoughtfully. "I learned most everything I know on the streets, not in an expensive private school. I doubt there's a single political issue we can agree on. You're standing on one side of the fence and I'm way over on the other. We're about as far apart as any two people could ever be. Socially. Economically. And every other way I could mention. We have no business even speaking to one another, and yet we sat down and shared a meal and talked for hours."

"I felt betrayed by that column."

"I know. I apologize, although the damage is already done. I guess I didn't realize it would offend you. That wasn't what I intended at all." He released a giant sigh and paused, as though collecting his thoughts. "After I left your place, I felt good. I can't remember a time I've enjoyed myself more. You're a charming, interesting—"

"You might have said that in your column!"

"I did, only you were obviously too upset to notice it. When I got home that night, I couldn't sleep. Every time I'd start to drift off, I'd think of something you'd said, and before I knew it I'd be grinning. Finally I got up and sat at my desk and started writing. The words poured out of me as fast as I could type them. The quality that impressed me the most about you is your honesty. There isn't a pretense in you, and the more I thought about that the more I realized how you've been cheated."

"And you decided it was your duty to point all this out—for everyone in town to read?"

"No, it wasn't. That's why I'm here. I admit I went further than I should have and came over to apologize."

"If you're telling me this to make me feel better, it isn't working." Her ego was rebounding somewhat, but he still had a lot of apologizing to do.

"To be honest, I didn't give the column a second thought until this afternoon, when someone in the office said I'd really done it now. If I was hoping to make peace with you, I'd failed. This friend said I was likely to get hit by the wrath of a woman scorned and suggested I run for cover."

"Rightly so!"

"Forgive me, Maryanne. It was arrogant in the extreme of me to publish that piece. If it'll help you feel any better, you can blast me to kingdom come in your next column. I solemnly promise I'll never write another word about you."

"Don't be so humble—it doesn't suit you," she muttered, gnawing on her lower lip. "Besides, I won't be able to print a rebuttal."

"Why not?"

"I don't plan on working for the *Review* any longer, or at least not after tomorrow." The idea seemed to emerge fully formed; until that moment she hadn't known exactly what she was going to say.

The silence following her words was fraught with tension. "What do you mean?"

"Don't act so surprised. I'm quitting the paper."

"What? Why?" Kramer had been standing during their whole conversation, but he suddenly seemed to find it necessary to sit. He slowly lowered himself on the sofa, his face pale and tight. "You're overreacting! There's no need to do anything so drastic."

"There's every need. You said so yourself. You told me I've been cheated, that if I'm even half as good a reporter as I think I am, I would have got this 'plum position' on my own. I'm just agreeing with you."

He nodded stiffly.

"As painful as this is to admit, especially to you," she went on, "you're right. My family is wonderful, but they've never allowed me to fall flat on my face. Carol Riverside is the one who deserved the chance to write that column. She's been with the paper for five years— I'd only been there five minutes. But because my name is Simpson and because my father made a simple phone call, I was given the job. Carol was cheated. She should have been furious. Instead, she was kind and helpful." Maryanne sat down next to Kramer and propped her feet on the coffee table. "And maybe worse than what happened to Carol is what happened to me as a result of being handed this job. What you wrote about my wondering if I had what it takes to make it as a journalist hit too close to home. All my life my father's been there to tell me I can be anything I want to be and then he promptly arranges it for me."

"Quitting the *Review* isn't going to change that,"
Kramer argued. "Come on, Annie, you're taking this
all too seriously."

"Nothing you say is going to change my mind,"
Maryanne informed him primly. "The time has come
for me to cut myself loose and sink or swim on my
own."

Her mind was galloping ahead, adjusting to the
coming changes. For the first time since she'd read
Kramer's column that afternoon, she experienced the
beginnings of excitement. She glanced around the
apartment as another thought struck her. "Naturally
I'll have to move out of this place."

"Are you going back to New York?"

"Heavens, no!" she declared, unaccountably thrilled
at the reluctance she heard in his voice. "I love Seattle."

"Listen to me, would you? You're leaping into the
deep end, you don't know how to swim and the lifeguard's off duty."

Maryanne barely heard Kramer, mainly because she
didn't like what he was saying. How like a man to ignite a bonfire and then rush to put out the flames. "The
first thing I need to worry about is finding another
job," she announced. "A temporary one, of course.
I'm going to continue writing, but I don't think I'll be
able to support myself on that, not at first, anyway."

"If you insist on this folly, you could always free-
lance for the *Sun.*"

Maryanne discounted that suggestion with a shake of
her head. "I'd come off looking like a traitor."

"I suppose you're right." His eyebrows drew together as he frowned.

"You know what else I'm going to do?" She shifted her position, tucking her legs beneath her. "I've got this trust fund that provides a big interest payment every month. That's what I've been using to pay my bills. You and I both know I couldn't afford this place on what I make at the paper. I'm not going to touch those interest payments and I'll live solely on what I earn."

"I . . . wouldn't do that right away, if I were you."

"Why not?"

"You just said you were quitting your job." Kramer sounded uneasy. "I can see that I've started something of an avalanche here, and I'm beginning to feel mildly concerned."

"Where do you live?"

"Capitol Hill. Listen, if you're serious about moving, you need to give some thought to what kind of neighborhood you're getting into. Seattle's a great town, don't get me wrong, but like any other place we have our problem areas." He hesitated. "Annie, I don't feel good about this."

"No one's ever called me Annie before." Her eyes smiled into his. "What do you pay for rent?"

With his hands buried deep in his pants pockets, he mumbled something under his breath, then mentioned a figure that was one-third of what she was currently dishing out every month.

"That's more than reasonable."

Surprise flashed in his eyes, and Maryanne smiled again. "If you're so concerned about my finding the right neighborhood, then you pick one for me. Anyplace, I don't care. Just remember, you're the one who got me into this."

"Don't remind me." Kramer's frown darkened.

"I may not have appreciated what you said about me in your column," Maryanne said slowly, "but I'm beginning to think good things might come of it."

"I'm beginning to think I should be dragged to the nearest tree and hanged," Kramer grumbled.

"HI." MARYANNE SLIPPED into the booth opposite Kramer at the greasy spoon called Mom's Place. She smiled, feeling like a child on a grand adventure. Perhaps she *was* going off the deep end, as Kramer had so adamantly claimed the day before. Perhaps, but she doubted it. Everything felt incredibly right.

Once the idea of living on her own—on income she earned herself, from a job she'd been hired for on her own merits—had taken hold in her mind, it had fast gained momentum. She could work days and write nights. The arrangement was perfect.

"Did you do it?"

"I handed in my notice first thing this morning," she said, reaching for the menu. Kramer had insisted on meeting her for a late lunch and suggested this greasy spoon with its faded neon sign that flashed Home Cooking. She had the impression he ate there regularly.

"I talked to the managing editor first thing this morning and told him I was leaving."

"I don't imagine he took kindly to that," Kramer muttered, lifting a white ceramic mug half-full of coffee. He'd been wearing a frown from the moment she'd entered the diner. She had the feeling it was the same one he'd left her apartment with the night before, but it had deepened slightly since she'd last seen him.

"Larry wasn't too upset, but I don't think he appreciated my suggestion that Carol Riverside take over the column, because he said something I'd rather not repeat about how he was the one who'd do the promoting and demoting, not me, no matter what my name was.''

Kramer took a sip of coffee and grinned. ''I'd bet he'd like my head if it could be arranged, and frankly, I don't blame him.''

''Don't worry, I didn't mention your name or the fact that your column was what led to my decision.''

Maryanne doubted Kramer even heard her. ''I'm regretting that column more with each passing minute. Are you sure I can't talk you out of this?''

''I'm sure.''

He sighed and he shook his head. ''How'd the job hunting go?''

The waitress came by, automatically placing a filled mug of coffee in front of Maryanne. She fished a pad from the pocket of her pink apron. ''Are you ready to order?''

''I'll have a turkey sandwich on rye, no sprouts, a diet soda and a side of potato salad,'' Maryanne said with a smile, handing her the menu.

''You don't need to worry, we don't serve sprouts here,'' she said, scribbling down the order.

''I'll have the chili, Barbara,'' Kramer said. The waitress nodded and strolled away from the booth. ''I was asking how your job hunting went,'' Kramer reminded Maryanne.

''I found one!''

''Where? And what will you be doing? And for how much?''

''You're beginning to sound like my father.''

''I'm beginning to *feel* like your father. Annie, you're a babe in the woods. You don't have a clue what you're getting involved in. Heaven knows I've tried to talk some sense into you, but you refused to listen. And, as you so delight in reminding me, I'm the one responsible for all this."

"Stop blaming yourself." Maryanne reached across the table for her water glass. "I'm grateful, I honestly am—though, trust me, I never thought I'd be saying that. But what you wrote was true. By insulting me, you've given me the initiative to make a name for myself without Dad's help and—"

He closed his eyes. "Just answer the question."

"Oh, about the job. It's for a . . . service company. It looks like it'll work out great. Actually, I didn't think I'd have any chance of getting hired, since I don't have much experience, but they took that into consideration. You see, it's a new company and they can't afford to pay much. Everyone seems friendly and helpful. The only drawback is my salary and the fact that I won't be working a lot of hours at first. In fact, the money is a lot less than I was earning at the paper. But I expect to be able to sell a couple of articles soon. I'll get along all right once I learn to budget."

"How much less than the paper?"

"If I tell you, you'll only get angry." His scowl said he'd be even angrier if she didn't tell him. From the way he was glaring at her, Maryanne knew she'd reached the limits of his patience. She muttered the amount and promptly lowered her gaze.

"You aren't taking the job," Kramer said flatly.

"Yes, I am. It's the best I could do for now. Besides, it's only temporary. It isn't all that easy to find work, you know. I must have talked to fifteen companies today. No one seemed too impressed with my double degree in Early American History and English. I wanted to find employment where I can use my writing skills, but that didn't happen, so I took this job.''

''Annie, you won't be able to live on so little.''

''I realize that. I've got a list of the community newspapers and I'm going to contact them about doing free-lance work. I figure between the writing and my job, I'll do all right.''

''Exactly *what* will you be doing?'' he demanded.

''Cleaning,'' she mumbled under her breath.

''What did you say?''

''I'm working for Rent-A-Maid.''

''Dear Lord,'' Kramer groaned. ''I hope you're kidding.''

''Get your mind out of the gutter, Adams. I'm going to work six hours a day cleaning offices and spend the rest of the time doing research for my articles. Oh, and before I forget, I gave your name as a reference.''

''You're going to go back and tell whoever hired you that you're terribly sorry, but you won't be able to work there, after all,'' Kramer announced, and the hard set of his mouth brooked no argument.

Maryanne was saved from having to tell him she had no intention of quitting, because the waitress, bless her heart, appeared with their orders at precisely that moment.

''Now what about an apartment?'' Maryanne asked. After his comment about living in a safe neighborhood, she was more than willing to let him locate one for her. ''Have you had a chance to check into that for me?''

''I hope you didn't give your notice at The Seattle.''

Swallowing a bite of her sandwich, Maryanne nodded eagerly. ''First thing this morning. I told them I'd

be out by the fifteenth, which in case you were unaware of it, happens to be early next week."

"You shouldn't have done that."

"I can't afford the place! And I won't be able to eat
in restaurants everyday or take cabs or buy things
whenever I want them." She smiled proudly as she said
it. Money had never been a problem in her life—it had
sometimes been an issue, but never a problem. She felt
invigorated just thinking about her new status.

"Will you stop grinning at me like that?" Kramer
burst out.

"Sorry, it's sort of a novelty to say I can't afford
something, that's all," she explained. "It actually feels
kind of good."

"In a couple of weeks it's going to feel like hell."
Kramer's face spelled out apprehension and gloom.

"Then I'll learn that for myself." She noticed he
hadn't touched his meal. "Go ahead and eat your chili
before it gets cold."

"I've lost my appetite." He immediately contra-
dicted himself by reaching for a small bottle of hot
sauce and dousing the chili with several hard shakes.

"Now did you or did you not find me a furnished
studio apartment to look at this afternoon?" Maryanne pressed.

"I found one. It's nothing like you're used to, so be
prepared. I'll take you there once we're finished lunch."

"Tell me about it," Maryanne said eagerly.

"There's one main room, small kitchen, smaller
bathroom, tiny closet, no dishwasher." He paused as if
he expected her to jump to her feet and tell him the
whole thing was off.

"Go on," she said, reaching for her soda.

"The floors are pretty worn but they're hardwood."

"That'll be nice." She didn't know if she'd ever lived in a place that didn't have carpeting, but she'd adjust.

"The furniture's solid enough. It's old and weighs about a ton, but I don't know how comfortable it is."

"I'm sure it'll be fine. I'll be working just about everyday, so I can't see that there'll be a problem," Maryanne returned absently. As soon as she'd spoken, she realized her mistake.

Kramer stabbed his spoon into the chili. "You seem to have forgotten you're resuming your job hunt. You won't be working for Rent-A-Maid, and that's final."

"You sound like a parent again. I'm old enough to know what I can and can't do, and I'm going to take that job whether you like it or not, and *that's final.*"

His eyes narrowed. "We'll see."

"Yes, we will," she retorted. Kramer might be an astute journalist, but there were several things he had yet to learn about her, and one of them was her stubborn streak. The thought produced a small smile as she realized she was thinking of him in a way that suggested a long-term friendship. He was right when he said they stood on opposite sides of the fence on most issues. He was also right when he claimed they had no business being friends. Nevertheless, Kramer Adams was the most intriguing man she'd ever known.

Once they'd finished their meal, Kramer reached for the bill, but Maryanne insisted on splitting it. He clearly wasn't pleased about that but let it pass. Apparently he wasn't going to argue with her, which suited Maryanne just fine. He escorted her to his car, parked outside the diner, and Maryanne slid inside, absurdly pleased that he'd cleaned up the front seat for her.

Kramer hesitated when he joined her, his hands on the steering wheel. "Are you sure you want to go through with this?"

"Positive."

"I was afraid you were going to say that." His mouth twisted. "I can't believe I'm aiding and abetting this nonsense."

"You're my friend, and I'm grateful."

Without another word, he started the engine.

"Where's the apartment?" Maryanne asked as the car progressed up the steep Seattle hills. "I mean, what neighborhood?"

"Capitol Hill."

"Oh, how nice. Isn't that the same part of town you live in?" It wasn't all that far from The Seattle, either, which meant she'd still have the same telephone exchange. Maybe she could even keep her current number.

"Yes," he muttered. He didn't seem to be in the mood for conversation and kept his attention centered on his driving, instead. He pulled into a parking lot behind an eight-story post-World War II brick building. "The apartment's on the fourth floor."

"That'll be fine." She climbed out of the car and stared at the old structure. The garbage dumpster was backed against the wall and full to overflowing. Maryanne had to step around it before entering by a side door. Apparently there was no elevator, and by the time they reached the fourth floor, she was so winded she couldn't have found the breath to complain, anyway.

"The manager gave me the key," Kramer explained as he paused in the hallway and unlocked the second door on the right. Kramer wasn't even breathing deeply, while Maryanne was leaning against the wall, dragging deep breaths into her oxygen-starved lungs.

Kramer opened the door and waved her in. "As I said, it's not much."

Maryanne walked inside and was immediately struck by the sparseness of the furnishings. One overstuffed sofa and one end table with a lamp on a dull stained wood floor. She blinked, squared her shoulders and forced a smile to her lips. "It's perfect."

"You honestly think you can live here after The Seattle?" He sounded incredulous.

"Yes, I do," she said with a determination that would have made generations of Simpsons proud. "How far away is your place?"

Kramer walked over to the window, his back to her. He exhaled sharply before he announced, "I live in the apartment next door."

CHAPTER THREE

"I DON'T NEED a baby-sitter," Maryanne protested. She had some trouble maintaining the conviction in her voice. In truth, she was pleased to learn that Kramer's apartment was next door, and her heart did a little jig all its own.

Kramer turned away from the window. His mouth was set in a thin straight line, as if he was going against his better judgment in arranging this. "That night at the radio station," he mumbled softly. "I knew it then."

"Knew what?"

Slowly, he shook his head, apparently lost in his musings. "I took one look at you and deep down inside I heard a small voice cry out, 'Here comes trouble.'"

Despite his fierce look, Maryanne laughed.

"Like a fool I ignored it, although Lord only knows how I could have."

"You're not blaming me for all this, are you?" Maryanne asked, placing her hands on her hips, prepared to do battle. "In case you've forgotten, you're the one who invited yourself to dinner that night. Then you got me all mellow with wine—"

"You were the one who brought out the bottle. You can't blame me for that." He was muttering again, and he buried his hands deep in the pockets of his raincoat.

"I was only being a good hostess."

"All right, all right, I get the picture," he said through clenched teeth, shaking his head again. "I was the one stupid enough to write that column afterward. I'd give a week's pay to take it all back now. No, make that a month's pay. This is the last time," he vowed, "that I'm ever going to set the record straight. Any record." He jerked his hand from his pocket and stared at it for several moments.

Maryanne crossed to the large stuffed sofa covered with fading chintz fabric and ran her hand along the armrest. It was nearly threadbare in places and nothing like the supple white leather of her sofa at The Seattle. "I wish you'd stop worrying about me. I'm not as fragile as I look."

Kramer snickered softly. "A dust ball could bowl you over."

A ready argument sprang to her lips, but she quickly swallowed it. "I'll take the apartment, but I want it understood, right now, that you have no responsibilities toward me. I'm a big girl and I'll manage perfectly well on my own. I have in the past and I'll continue to do so in the future."

Kramer didn't respond immediately. Instead he grumbled something she couldn't hear. He seemed to be doing a lot of that since he'd met her. Maybe it was a long established habit, but somehow she doubted it.

Kramer drove her back to The Seattle, and the whole way there Maryanne could hardly contain a feeling of delight. For the first time, she was taking control of her own life. Kramer, however, was all too obviously experiencing no such enthusiasm.

"Do I need to sign anything for the apartment? What about a deposit?"

"You can do that later. You realize this studio apartment is the smallest one in the entire building. My own apartment is three times that size."

"Would you stop worrying," Maryanne told him. A growing sense of purpose filled her, and a keen exhilaration unlike anything she'd ever felt.

Kramer pulled into the circular driveway at her building. "Do you want to come up for a few minutes?" she asked.

His dark eyes widened as if she'd causally suggested they play a round of Russian roulette. "You've got to be kidding."

She wasn't.

He held up both hands. "No way. Before long, you'll be serving wine and we'll be talking like old friends. Then I'll go home thinking about you, and before I know how it happened—" He stopped abruptly, as if he'd already said too much. "No, thanks."

"Goodbye then," she said, disappointed. "I'll see you later."

"Right. Later." But the way he said it suggested that if he didn't stumble upon her for a decade or two, it would be fine with him.

Maryanne climbed out of his car and was about to close the door when she hesitated. "Kramer?"

"Now what?" he barked.

"Thank you," she said softly.

Predictably, he started mumbling and drove off the instant she closed the door. In spite of his sour mood, Maryanne found herself smiling.

Once inside her apartment, she was immediately struck by the contrast between this apartment at The Seattle and the place Kramer had shown her. One was gray, cramped and dingy, the other polished and spacious and elegant. Her mind's eye went over the dreary apartment on Capitol Hill, and she felt a growing sense of excitement as she thought of different inexpensive ways to bring it color and character. She'd certainly faced challenges before, but never one quite like this. Instinctively she knew there would be real satisfaction in decorating that place with her newly limited resources.

Turning her new apartment into a home was the least of her worries, however. She had yet to tell her parents that she'd quit her job. Their reaction was as predictable as Kramer's.

The phone seemed to draw her. Slowly she walked across the room toward it, sighing deeply. Her fingers closed tightly around the receiver. Before she could change her mind, she closed her eyes, punched out the number and waited.

Her mother answered almost immediately.

"I was sitting at my desk," Muriel Simpson explained. She sounded delighted to hear from Maryanne. "How's Seattle? Are you still as fascinated with the Northwest as you were before?"

"More than ever," Maryanne answered without a pause; what she didn't say was that part of her fascination was now because of Kramer.

"I'm pleased you like it so well, but I don't mind telling you, sweetie, I miss you something dreadful."

"I haven't lived at home for years," Maryanne reminded her mother.

"I know, but you were so much closer to home in Manhattan than you are now. I can't join you for lunch the way I did last year."

"Seattle's lovely. I hope you'll visit me soon." But not too soon, she prayed.

"Sometime this spring, I promise," Muriel replied. "I was afraid once you'd settled there, all that rain would get you down."

"Mother, honestly, New York City has more annual rainfall than Seattle."

"I know, dear, but in New York the rain all comes in a few days. In Seattle it drizzles for weeks on end, or so I've heard."

"It's not so bad." Maryanne had been far too busy to pay much attention to the weather. Gathering her courage, she forged ahead. "The reason I called is that I've got a bit of exciting news for you."

"You're madly in love and want to get married."

Muriel Simpson was looking forward to grandchildren and had been ever since Maryanne's graduation from college. Both her brothers, Mark and Sean, were several years younger, so Maryanne knew the responsibility had fallen on her. For the past couple of years they'd been introducing her to suitable young men.

"It's nothing that dramatic," Maryanne said, then losing her courage, she crossed her fingers behind her back and blurted out, "I've got a special assignment... for the, uh, paper." The lie nearly stuck in her throat.

"A special assignment?"

All right, she was stretching the truth about as far as it would go, and she hated doing it. But she had no choice. Kramer's reaction would look tame compared to her parents' if they ever found out she was working as a janitor. Rent-A-Maid gave it a fancy name, but basically she'd been hired to clean. It wasn't a glamorous job, nor was it profitable, but it was honest work and she needed something to tide her over until she made a name for herself in her chosen field.

"What kind of special assignment?"

"It has to do with work." Maryanne decided it was best to let her family assume the "assignment" was with the newspaper. She wasn't happy about this, in fact she felt downright depressed to be misleading her mother this way, but she dared not hint at what she'd actually be doing. The only comfort she derived was from the prospect of showing them her published work in a month or two.

"It's not anything dangerous, is it?"

"Oh heavens, no," Maryanne said, forcing a light laugh. "But I'm going to be involved in it for several weeks, so I won't be mailing you any of my columns, at least not for a while. I didn't want you to wonder when you didn't hear from me."

"Will you be traveling?"

"A little." Only a few city blocks as a matter of fact, but she couldn't very well say so. "Once everything's completed, I'll get in touch with you."

"You won't even be able to phone?" Her mother's voice carried a hint of concern.

Not often, at least not on her budget, Maryanne realized regretfully.

"Of course I'll phone," she hurried to assure her mother. She didn't often partake in subterfuge, and being new to the game she was making everything up as she went along. She hoped her mother would be trusting enough to accept her at her word.

"Speaking of your columns, dear, tell me what happened with that dreadful reporter who was harassing you earlier in the month."

"Dreadful reporter?" Maryanne repeated uncertainly. "Oh," she said with a flash of insight. "You mean Kramer."

"That's his name?" Her mother's voice rose indignantly. "I hope he's at least stopped using that column of his to irritate you."

"It was all in good fun, Mother." All right, he *had* irritated her, but Maryanne was willing to forget their earlier pettiness. "We're friends now. In fact, I like him quite a lot."

"Friends," her mother echoed softly. Slowly. "I don't suppose your newfound friend is married, is he? You know your father and I started our own relationship at odds with each other, don't you?"

"Mother, honestly. Stop matchmaking."

"Just answer me one thing. Is he married or not?"

"Not. He's in his early thirties and he's handsome." A noticeable pause followed the description. "Mother?"

"You're attracted to him, aren't you?"

Maryanne wasn't sure if she should admit it, but on the other hand, she'd already given herself away. "Yes," she said stiffly, "I am . . . a little. There's a lot to like about him, even though we don't always agree. He's very talented. I've never read a column of his that didn't make me smile—and think. He's got this, um, interesting sense of humor."

"So it seems. Has he asked you out?"

"Not yet." *But he will,* her heart told her.

"Give him time." Muriel Simpson's voice had lowered a notch or two, and again Maryanne could almost hear the wheels turning in her mother's head. "Now, sweetie, before we hang up, I want you to tell me some more about this special assignment of yours."

They talked for a few minutes longer, and Maryanne surprised herself at the way she managed to avoid answering her mother's direct questions. She hated this subterfuge, and she hated the guilt she felt afterward. She tried to reason it away by reminding herself that her motives were good. If her parents knew what she was planning, they'd be sick with worry. But she couldn't remain their little girl forever. She had something to prove, and for the first time she was going to compete like a real contender—without her father standing on the sidelines, bribing the judges.

MARYANNE DIDN'T HEAR from Kramer for the next three days, and she was getting anxious. At the end of the week, she'd be finished at the *Review*; the following Monday she'd be starting at Rent-A-Maid. To her delight, Carol Riverside was appointed as her replacement. The look the managing editor tossed Maryanne's way suggested he'd given Carol the job not because of her recommendation, but despite it.

"I'm still not convinced you're doing the right thing," Carol told her over lunch on Maryanne's last day at the paper.

"But *I'm* convinced, and that's what's important," Maryanne returned. "Why is it everyone's so afraid I'm going to fall flat on my face?"

"It's not that, exactly."

"Then what is it?" she pressed. "I don't think Kramer stopped grumbling from the moment I announced I was quitting the paper, finding a job and moving out on my own."

"And well he should grumble!" Carol declared righteously. "He's the one who started this whole thing. You're such a nice girl. I can't see you getting mixed up with the likes of him."

Maryanne had a sneaking suspicion her friend wasn't saying this out of loyalty to the newspaper. "Mixed up with the likes of him? Is there something I don't know about Seattle's favorite journalist?''

"Kramer Adams may be the most popular newspaper writer in town, but he's got a biting edge to him. Oh, he's witty and talented, I'll give him that, but he has this scornful attitude that makes me want to shake him till he rattles."

"I realize he's a bit cynical."

"He's a good deal more than cynical. The problem is he's so darn entertaining that his attitude is easy to overlook. I'd like two minutes alone with that man just so I could set him straight. He had no business saying what he did about you in that 'My Evening with the Debutante' piece. Look where it's led!"

For that matter, Maryanne wouldn't mind spending two minutes alone with Kramer, either, but for an entirely different reason. The speed with which the thought entered her mind surprised her enough to produce a soft smile.

"Only this time his words came back to hit him in the face," Carol continued.

"Everything he wrote was true," Maryanne felt obliged to remind her friend. She hadn't been all that thrilled when he'd decided to share those truths with the entire western half of Washington state, but she couldn't fault his perceptions.

"Needless to say, I'm not as concerned with Kramer as I am with you," Carol said, gazing down at her sandwich. "I've seen that little spark in your eye when you talk about him, and frankly it worries me."

Maryanne immediately lowered her betraying eyes. "I'm sure you're mistaken. Kramer and I are friends, but that's the extent of it." She wasn't entirely sure

Kramer would even want to claim her as a friend; she rather suspected he thought of her as a nuisance.

"Perhaps it's friendship on his part, but it's a lot more on yours. I'm afraid you're going to fall in love with that scoundrel."

"That's crazy," Maryanne countered swiftly. "I've only just met him." Carol's gaze narrowed on her like a diamond drill bit and Maryanne sighed. "He intrigues me," she admitted, "but that's a long way from becoming emotionally involved with him."

"I can't help worrying about you. And, Maryanne, your falling in love with Kramer worries me more than the fact that you're cleaning offices or found yourself an apartment on Capitol Hill."

Maryanne swallowed tightly. "Kramer's a talented respected journalist. If I was going to fall in love with him, which I don't plan to do in the near future, but if I *did* fall for him, why would it be so tragic?"

"Because you're sweet and caring and he's so..." Carol paused and stared into space. "Because he's so scornful."

"True, but underneath that gruff exterior is a heart of gold. At least I think it's there," Maryanne joked.

"Maybe, but I doubt it," Carol went on. "Don't get me wrong—I respect Kramer's talent. It's his devil-may-care attitude that troubles me."

But it didn't trouble Maryanne. Not in the least. Perhaps that was what she found most appealing about him. Yet everything Carol said about Kramer was true. He did tend to be cynical and a bit sardonic, but he was also intuitive, reflective and, despite Carol's impression to the contrary, considerate.

Since it was her last day at the paper, Maryanne spent a few extra minutes saying goodbye to her coworkers.

Most were sorry to see her go. There had been a fair amount of resentment directed at her when she'd first arrived, but her hard work seemed to have won over all but the most skeptical doubters.

On impulse, Maryanne stopped off at the diner where Kramer had met her earlier in the week, hoping he'd be there. Her heart flew to her throat when she saw him sitting in a booth by the window, a book propped open in front of him. He didn't look up when she walked in.

Nor did he notice her when she approached his booth. Without waiting for an invitation, she slid in across from him.

"Hi," she murmured, keeping her voice low and secretive. "Here comes trouble to plague you once more."

Slowly, with obvious reluctance, Kramer dragged his gaze from the novel. Another mystery, Maryanne noted. "What are you doing here, Trouble?"

"Looking for you."

"Why? Have you thought up any other ways to test my patience? How about walking a tightrope between two skyscrapers? That sounds right up your alley."

"I hadn't heard from you in the past couple of days." She paused, hoping he'd pick up the conversation. "I thought there was something I should do about the apartment. Sign a lease, give the manager a deposit, that sort of thing."

"Annie—"

"I hope you realize I don't even know the address. I only saw it that one time."

"I told you not to worry about it."

"But I don't want anyone else to rent it."

"They won't." He laid the book aside just as the waitress appeared carrying a glass of water and a menu. Maryanne recognized her from the other day. "Hello,

Barbara,'' she said, reading the woman's plastic name tag. ''What's the special for the day? Mr. Adams owes me a meal and I think I'll collect it while I've got the chance.'' She waited for him to ask her what she was talking about, but he apparently remembered his promise of dinner to pay her back for the Irish stew he'd eaten at her house the first evening they'd met.

''Cabbage rolls, with soup or salad,'' Barbara said, reaching for her pad and pencil while Maryanne quickly scanned the menu.

''I'll have a cheeseburger and a chocolate shake,'' Maryanne decided.

Barbara grinned. ''I'll make sure it comes up with Mr. Adams's order.''

''Thanks,'' she said, handing her back the menu. Barbara sauntered off toward the kitchen, scribbling on her order pad as she walked.

''It was my last day at the paper,'' Maryanne announced.

''I'll ask you one more time—are you sure you want to go through with this?'' Kramer demanded. ''Hell, I never thought for a moment you'd want that apartment. Damn it all, but you're a stubborn woman.''

''Of course I'm taking the apartment.''

''That's what I thought.'' He closed his eyes briefly. ''What did the Rent-A-Maid agency say when you told them you wouldn't be taking the job?''

Purposely Maryanne stared out the window. ''Nothing.''

He cocked an eyebrow. ''Nothing?''

''What could they say?'' she asked, trying to ignore the doubt reflected in his eyes. Maybe she was getting good at this lie-telling business, which wasn't a comforting thought. The way she'd misled her mother still bothered her.

Kramer drew one hand across his face. "You didn't tell them, did you? Apparently you intend to play the Cinderella role to the hilt."

"And you intend to play the role of my wicked stepmother to perfection."

He didn't say anything for a long moment. "Is there a part in that fairy tale where Cinderella gets locked in a closet for her own good?"

"Why?" she couldn't resist asking. "Is that what you're going to do to me?"

"Don't tempt me."

"I wish you had more faith in me."

"I do have faith in you. I have faith that you're going to make my life hell for the next several months while you go about proving yourself. Heaven knows what possessed me to write that stupid column, but trust me, there hasn't been a minute since it hit the streets that I haven't regretted it. Not a single minute."

"But—"

"Now you insist on moving into the apartment next to mine. That's just great. Wonderful. Whatever peace I have in my life will be completely and utterly destroyed."

"That's not true!" Maryanne cried. "Besides, I'd like to remind you, you're the one who found that apartment not me. I have no intention of pestering you."

"Like I said, I figured just seeing the apartment would be enough to put you off. Now I won't have a moment to myself again. I know it, and you know it." His eyes were darker and more brooding than she'd ever seen them. "I wasn't kidding when I said you were trouble."

"All right," Maryanne said, doing her best to disguise her crushing sense of defeat. "It's obvious you never expected me to take the place. I suppose you arranged it to look as bleak as you could. Don't worry, I'll find somewhere else to live. Another apartment as far away from you as I can possibly get." She was out of the booth so fast, so intent on escaping, that she nearly collided with Barbara.

"What about your cheeseburger?" the waitress asked.

Maryanne glanced at Kramer. "Wrap it up and give it to Mr. Adams. I've lost my appetite."

The tears that blurred her eyes only angered her more. Furious with herself for allowing Kramer's words to wound her, she hurried down the street, headed in the direction of the Seattle waterfront. It was growing dark, but she didn't care; she needed to vent some of her anger, and a brisk hike would serve that purpose nicely.

She wasn't concerned when she heard hard quick footsteps behind her. As the wind whipped at her, she shivered and drew her coat closer, tucking her hands in her pockets and hunching her shoulders forward.

First Carol had issued a warning, and now Kramer. Everyone seemed to believe she needed a keeper! They apparently considered her incompetent, and their doubts cut deeply into her pride.

Her head bowed against the force of the wind, she noticed a pair of male legs match steps with her own. She glanced up and discovered Kramer had joined her.

For the longest time, he said nothing. They were halfway down a deserted pier before he spoke. "I don't want you to find another apartment."

"I think it would be best if I did." He'd already told her she was nothing but trouble, and as if that wasn't bad enough, he implied she was going to be a constant nuisance in his life. She had no intention of pestering him. As far as she was concerned, he could live on the other side of town. That was what he wanted and that was what he was going to get.

"It isn't for the best," he argued.

"It is. We obviously rub each other the wrong way."

Kramer turned and gripped her by the shoulders. "The apartment's been cleaned. It's ready for you to move into anytime you want. The rent is reasonable and the neighborhood's a good one. As I recall, this whole ridiculous business between us started over an article about the lack of affordable housing. You're not going to find anyplace else, not with what you intend to live on."

"But you live next door!"

"I'm well aware of that."

Maryanne bristled. "I won't live beside a man who considers me a pest. And furthermore you still owe me dinner."

"I said you were trouble," he pointed out, ignoring her claim. "I didn't say you were a pest."

"You did so."

"I said you were going to destroy my peace—"

"Exactly."

"—of mind," he went on. He closed his eyes briefly and expelled a sharp frustrated sigh, then repeated, "You're going to destroy my peace of mind."

Maryanne wasn't sure she understood. She stared up at him, intrigued by the emotion she saw in his intense brown eyes.

"Why the hell should it matter if you live next door to me or in The Seattle?" he exclaimed. "My serenity was shot the minute I laid eyes on you."

"I don't understand," she said, surprised when her voice came out a raspy whisper. She continued to look up at him, trying to read his expression.

"You don't have a clue, do you?" he whispered. His fingers found their way into her hair as he lowered his mouth with heart-stopping slowness toward hers. "Heaven keep me from redheaded innocents."

But heaven apparently didn't receive the message, because even as he whispered the words, Kramer's arms were pulling her toward him. With a sigh of regret—or was it pleasure?—his mouth settled over hers. His kiss was light and undemanding, and despite the anger, despite his words, Maryanne felt herself melting.

With a soft sigh, she flattened her hands on his chest and slid them up to link behind his neck. She leaned against him, letting his strength support her, letting his warmth comfort her.

He pulled her even closer, wrapped his arms around her waist and half lifted her from the pier. Maryanne heard a low hungry moan; she wasn't sure if it came from Kramer or from her.

It didn't matter, she decided. Nothing mattered except this wonderful feeling of being cherished and loved and protected.

Over the years, Maryanne had been kissed by her share of men. She'd found the experience pleasant, but no one had ever set her on fire the way Kramer did now.

"See what I mean," he whispered unsteadily. "We're in trouble here. Big trouble."

CHAPTER FOUR

MARYANNE STOOD in the doorway of her new apartment, the key clenched tightly in her hand. She was embarking on her grand adventure, but now that she'd actually moved out of The Seattle she found her confidence a bit shaky.

Carol joined her, huffing and puffing as she staggered the last few steps down the narrow hallway. She sagged against the wall, panting to catch her breath.

"This place doesn't have an elevator?" she demanded, when she could speak.

"It's being repaired."

"That's what they always say."

Maryanne nodded, barely hearing her friend. Her heart in her throat, she inserted the key and turned the lock. The door stuck, so she used the force of one hip to dislodge it. The apartment was just as she remembered it: worn hardwood floors, the bulky faded furniture, the kitchen appliances that would soon be valuable antiques. But Maryanne saw none of that.

This was her new life.

She walked directly to the window and gazed out. "I've got a great view of Volunteer Park," she announced to her friend. She hadn't noticed it the day Kramer had shown her the apartment. "I had no idea the park was so close." She turned toward Carol, who was still standing in the threshold, her expression one of shock and dismay. "What's wrong?"

"Good heavens," Carol whispered. "You don't really intend on living here, do you?"

"It isn't so bad," Maryanne said with a smile, glancing around to be sure she hadn't missed anything. "I've got lots of ideas on how to decorate the place." She leaned back against the windowsill, where much of the dingy beige paint was chipped away to reveal an even dingier gray-green. "What it needs is a fresh coat of paint, something light and cheerful."

"It's not even half the size of your other place."

"There was a lot of wasted space at my apartment there." That might be true, Maryanne thought privately, but she wouldn't have minded bringing some of it with her.

"What about your neighbor?" Carol asked in a grudging voice. "He's the one who started this. The least he could do is offer a little help."

Straightening, Maryanne brushed the dust from her palms and looked away. "I didn't ask him to. In fact, I don't think he even knows when I was planning to move in."

Kramer was a subject Maryanne wanted to avoid. She hadn't talked to him since the night he'd followed her to the waterfront...the night he'd kissed her. He'd stopped off at The Seattle to leave the apartment key and a rental agreement with the doorman. Max had promptly delivered both. The implication was obvious; Kramer didn't want to see her and was, in fact, doing his best to avoid her.

Clearly he disapproved of the way things had developed on the pier that night. She supposed he didn't like kissing her. Then again, perhaps he did. Perhaps he liked it too much for his oft-lamented "peace of mind."

Maryanne knew how *she* felt about it. She couldn't sleep for two nights afterward. Every time she closed her eyes, the image of Kramer holding her in his arms danced through her mind like a waltzing couple from a 1940s' movie. She remembered the way he scowled down at her when he'd broken off the kiss and how he'd struggled to make light of the incident. And she remembered his eyes, so warm and gentle, telling her another story.

"Hey, lady, is this the place where I'm supposed to bring the boxes?" A lanky youth of about fourteen stood in the doorway, holding a large cardboard box in his arms.

"Y-yes," Maryanne said, recognizing the container as one of her own. "How'd you know to carry it up here?"

"Mr. Adams. He promised a bunch of us guys he'd play basketball with us if we'd help unload the truck."

"Oh. How nice. I'm Maryanne Simpson," she said, her heart warming at Kramer's unexpected thoughtfulness.

"Nice to meet you, lady. Now where do you want me to put this?"

Maryanne pointed toward the kitchen. "Just stack it in the corner over there." Before she finished, a second and third youth appeared, each hauling boxes.

Maryanne slipped past them and ran down the stairs to the parking lot behind the building. Kramer was standing in the back of Carol's husband's pickup, noisily distributing cardboard boxes and dire warnings. He didn't seem to notice her until she moved closer. When he did, he fell silent, a frown on his face.

"Hi," she said, feeling a little shy. "I came to thank you."

"You shouldn't have gone up and left the truck unattended," he barked, still frowning. "Anyone could have walked off with this."

"We just arrived."

"We?"

"Carol Riverside and me. She's upstairs trying to regain her breath. How long will it be before the elevator's fixed?"

"Not soon."

She nodded. Well, if he'd hoped to discourage her, she wasn't going to let him. So what if she had to walk up four flights of stairs everyday! It was wonderful aerobic exercise. In the past she'd paid good money to attend a health club for the same purpose.

Kramer returned to his task, lifting boxes and handing them to a long line of teenage boys. "I'm surprised you didn't have a moving company manage this for you."

"Are you kidding?" she joked. "Only rich people use moving companies."

"Is this all of it, or do you need to make a second trip?"

"This is it. Carol and I put everything else in storage earlier this morning. It's only costing me a few dollars a month. I have to be careful about money now, you know."

He scowled again. "When do you start with the cleaning company?"

"Monday morning."

Kramer placed his hands on his hips and glared down at her. "If you're really intending to accept that job—"

"Of course I am!"

"Then the first thing you'll need to do is ask for a raise."

"Oh, honestly, Kramer," she protested, walking backward. "I can't do that!"

"What you can't do is live on that amount of money, no matter how well you budget," he muttered. He leapt off the back of the truck as agilely as a cat. "Will you listen to me for once?"

"I am listening," she said. "It just so happens I don't agree. Quit worrying about me, would you? I'm going to be perfectly all right, especially once I start selling articles."

"I'm not a knight in shining armor, understand?" he shouted after her. "If you think I'll be racing to your rescue every time you're in trouble, then you need to think again."

"You're insulting me by even suggesting I'd accept your help." She tried to be angry with him but found it impossible. He might insist she was entirely on her own, but all the while he was lecturing her, he was doling out her boxes so that she wouldn't have to haul them up the stairs herself. Kramer might claim not to be a knight riding to her rescue, but he was behaving suspiciously like one.

Two hours later, Maryanne was alone in her new apartment for the first time. Hands on her hips, she stood in the middle of her living room and surveyed her kingdom. As she'd told Carol, it wasn't so bad. Boxes filled every bit of available space, but it wouldn't take her long to unpack and set everything in order.

She was grateful for the help Carol, Kramer and the neighborhood teenagers had given her, but now it was up to her. And she had lots of plans—she'd paint the walls and put up her pictures and buy some plants—to make this place cheerful and attractive. To turn it into a home.

It was dark before she was finished unpacking, and by that time she was both exhausted and hungry. Actually *famished* more adequately described her condition. Her hunger and exhaustion warred with each other: she was too tired to go out and buy herself something to eat, but too hungry to go to bed without eating. Making the decision about which she should do created a dilemma of startling proportions.

She'd just decided to make do with a bowl of cornflakes, sans the milk, when there was a loud knock at her door. She jerked it open to find Kramer standing there, wearing gray sweatpants and a sweat-soaked T-shirt. He held a basketball under one arm and clutched a large white paper sack in the other.

"Never open the door without knowing who's on the other side," he warned, walking directly into the apartment. He dropped the basketball on the sofa and placed his sack—obviously from a fast-food restaurant—on the coffee table. "That chain's there for a reason. Use it."

Maryanne was still standing at the door, inhaling the aroma of french fries and hamburgers. "Yes, your majesty."

"Don't get testy with me, either. I've just lost two years of my life on a basketball court. I'm too old for this, but luckily what I lack in youth I make up for in smarts."

"I see," she said, closing the door. For good measure she clipped the chain into place and turned the lock.

"A little show of appreciation would go a long way toward soothing my injuries," he told her, sinking onto the sofa. He rested his head against the cushion, eyes drifting shut.

"You can't be that smart, otherwise you'd have managed to get out of playing with boys twenty years younger than you," she said lightly. She had trouble keeping her eyes off the white sack on the scratched mahogany coffee table.

Kramer straightened, wincing as he did so. "I thought you might be hungry." He reached for the bag and removed a napkin-wrapped hamburger, which he tossed to her before taking a second for himself. Next he set out two cardboard cartons full of hot french fries and two cans of soda.

Maryanne sat down beside him, her hand pressed against her stomach to keep it from growling. "You'd better be careful," she said. "You're beginning to look suspiciously like that knight in shining armor."

"Don't kid yourself."

Maryanne was too hungry to waste time arguing. She devoured the hamburger and fries within minutes. Then she relaxed against the back of the sofa and sighed, content.

"I came to set some ground rules," Kramer explained. "The way I figure it, you and I need to get a few things straight. Clear the air, that sort of thing."

"Sure," she agreed. It sounded like a good idea, although she was fairly certain she knew what he wanted to talk about. "I've already promised not to pester you."

"Good. I intend to stay out of your way, too."

"Perfect." It didn't really sound all that wonderful, but it seemed to be what he wanted, so she didn't have much choice. "Anything else?"

Kramer hesitated. Then he leaned forward, resting his forearms on his knees. "Yes, one other thing." He glanced in her direction with a frown. "I don't think we should . . . you know, kiss again."

A short silence followed his words. At first Maryanne wasn't sure she'd heard him correctly.

"I realize talking about this may be embarrassing," Kramer continued, sounding as detached as if he'd introduced the subject of football scores. "I want you to know I'm suggesting this for your own good."

"I'm pleased to hear that." It demanded some effort not to mock him by rolling her eyes.

He nodded and cleared his throat, and Maryanne could see he wasn't nearly as indifferent as he wanted her to believe.

"There appears to be a certain amount of physical chemistry between us," he continued, avoiding even a glance in her direction. "I feel that the sooner we settle this, the less likelihood there'll be for misunderstandings later on. The last thing I need is for you to fall in love with me."

"That's it!" she cried, throwing up her arms. The ridiculousness of his comment revived her enough to allow her to indulge in some teasing. "The whole thing's off. If I can't have your heart and soul, then I'm leaving right now!"

"Damn it, Annie, this is nothing to joke about."

"Who's joking?" she asked. She made her voice sound absurdly melodramatic. "I knew the minute I walked into the radio station for the Celebrity Debate that if I couldn't taste your lips, there was nothing left to live for."

"If you're going to make a joke out of this, then you can forget the whole discussion." He vaulted to his feet and stuffed the wrappers from their burgers and fries into the empty sack with enough force to tear out the bottom. "I was hoping we could have a mature talk, one adult to another, but that's obviously beyond you."

"Don't get so bent out of shape," she said, trying not to smile. "Sit down before you do something silly, like leave in a huff. We both know you'll regret it." She didn't know anything of the sort, but it sounded good.

He complied grudgingly, but he stared past her, training his eyes on the darkened window.

Maryanne got stiffly to her feet, every muscle and joint protesting. "It seems to me that you're presuming a good deal with this hands-off decree," she said with all the dignity she could muster. "What makes you think I'd even *want* you to kiss me again?"

A slow cocky grin teased the corners of his mouth. "A man can tell. My biggest fear is that you're going to start thinking things I never meant you to think. Eventually you'd end up getting hurt. I intend to make damn sure nothing romantic develops between us. Understand?"

"You think my head's in the clouds when it comes to you?"

"That's right. You're a sweet kid, stubborn and idealistic, but nonetheless naive. One kiss told me you've got a romantic soul, and frankly, I don't want you fluttering those pretty blue eyes at me and dreaming of babies and a white picket fence. You and I are about as different as two people can get."

"Different?" To Maryanne's way of thinking, she had more in common with Kramer Adams than with any other man she'd ever dated.

"That's right. You come from this rich upstanding family—"

"Stop!" she cried. "Don't say another word about our economic differences. They're irrelevant. If you're looking for excuses, find something else."

"I don't need excuses. It'd never work between us and I want to make certain neither of us is ever tempted to try. If you want someone to teach you about being a woman, look elsewhere."

His words were like a slap across the face. "Naturally a man of your vast romantic experience gets plenty of requests." She turned away, so angry she couldn't keep still. "As for being afraid I might fall in love with you, let me assure you right now there's absolutely no chance of it. In fact, I think you should be more concerned about falling for me!" Her voice was gaining strength and conviction with every word. The man had such colossal nerve. At one time she might have found herself attracted to him, but that passed the minute he walked in her door and opened his mouth.

"Don't kid yourself," he argued. "You're halfway in love with me already. I can see it in your eyes."

Damn those expressive eyes of hers. Carol had said something about her eyes revealing what she felt for Kramer, too.

Maryanne whirled around, intent on composing a suitably sarcastic retort, away from his searching gaze. But before any mocking words could pass her lips, a sharp pain shot through her neck, an ache so intense it brought immediate tears to her eyes. She must have moved too quickly, too carelessly.

Her hands flew to the back of her neck.

Kramer was instantly on his feet. "What's wrong?"

"Nothing," she mumbled, easing her way back to the sofa. She sat down, hand still pressed to her neck, waiting a moment before slowly rotating her head, wanting to test the extent of her injury. Quickly, she realized her mistake.

"Annie," Kramer demanded, kneeling in front of her, "what is it?"

"I . . . don't know. I moved wrong, I guess."

His hands replaced hers. "You've got a crick in your neck?"

"If I do, it's all your fault. You say the most ridiculous things."

"I know." His voice was as gentle as his hands. He began to knead softly, his fingers tenderly massaging the tightened muscles.

"I'm all right."

"Of course you are," he whispered. "Just close your eyes and relax."

"I can't." How could he possibly expect her to do that when he was so close, so warm and sensual? He was fast making a lie of all her protestations.

"Yes, you can," he said, his voice low and seductive. He leaned over her, his face, his lips, scant inches from hers. His hands were working the tightness from her neck and shoulders and at the same time creating a dizzying heated sensation that extended to the tips of her fingers and the soles of her feet.

She sighed and clasped his wrist with both hands, wanting to stop him before she made a fool of herself by swaying toward him or doing something equally suggestive. "I think you should stop. Let me rephrase that. I *know* you should stop."

"I know I should, too," he admitted quietly. "Remember what I said earlier?"

"You mean the hands-off policy?"

"Yes." She could hardly hear him. "Let's delay it for a day—what do you think?"

At that moment, clear organized thought was something of a problem. "W-whatever you think is best."

"Oh, I know what's best," he whispered. "Unfortunately that doesn't seem to make a damn bit of difference right now."

She couldn't recall when it happened, but her hands seemed to have left his wrists and were splayed across the front of his T-shirt. His chest felt rigid and muscular; his heart beneath her palms pounded hard and fast. She wondered if her own pulse was keeping time with his.

With infinite slowness, Kramer lowered his mouth to hers. Maryanne's eyes drifted closed of their own accord and she moaned, holding back a small cry of welcome. His touch was even more compelling than she remembered. Kramer must have felt something similar, because his groan followed, an echo of hers.

He kissed her again and again. Maryanne wanted more, but he resisted giving in to her desires—or his own. It was as if he'd decided a few kisses were of little consequence and wouldn't seriously affect either one of them.

Wrong. Maryanne wanted to shout it at him, but couldn't.

His mouth left hers and blazed a fiery trail of kisses across her sensitized skin. His lips brushed her throat, under her chin to the vulnerable hollow. Only minutes earlier, moving her neck without pain had been impossible; now she did so freely, turning it, arching, asking—no, demanding—that he kiss her again the way he had that night at the waterfront.

Kramer complied, and he seemed to do it willingly, surrendering the battle. He groaned anew and the sound came from deep in his throat. His fingers tangled in the thick strands of her hair as his mouth rushed back to hers.

Maryanne was experiencing a renewal of her own. She felt as if she had lain dormant and was bursting to life, like a flower struggling out of winter snows into the light and warmth of spring.

All too soon, Kramer pulled away from her. His eyes met and held hers. She knew her eyes were filled with questions, but his gave her no answers.

He pulled away and abruptly stood.

"Kramer," she said, shocked that he would leave her so brusquely.

He looked back at her and she saw it then. The regret. A regret tinged with compassion. "You're so exhausted you can barely sit up. Go to bed and we'll both forget this ever happened. Understand?"

Too stunned to reply, she nodded. Maybe Kramer could forget it, but she knew she wouldn't.

"Lock the door after me. And next time don't be so eager to find out who's knocking. There isn't any doorman here."

Once more she nodded. She got up and followed him to the door, holding it open.

"Damn it, Annie, don't look at me like that."

"Like what?"

"Like that," he accused, then slowly shook his head as if to clear his thoughts. He rubbed his face and sighed, then pressed his knuckle under her chin. "The two of us are starting over first thing tomorrow. There won't be any more of this." But even as he was speaking, he was leaning forward to gently brush her mouth with his.

IT WAS THE SOUND of Kramer furiously pounding away on his electric typewriter—a heavy, outdated office model—that woke Maryanne the following morning. She yawned loudly, stretching her arms high above her head, arching her back. Her first night in her new apartment and she'd slept like a rock. The sofa, which opened into a queen-size sleeper, was lumpy and soft, nearly swallowing her up, but she'd been too exhausted to care.

Kramer's fierce typing continued most of the day. Maryanne hadn't expected to see him, so she wasn't disappointed when she didn't. He seemed determined to avoid her and managed it successfully for most of the week.

Since she'd promised not to make a nuisance of herself, Maryanne stayed out of his way, too. She started work at the cleaning company and wrote three articles in five days, often staying up late into the night.

The work for Rent-A-Maid was backbreaking and arduous. She spent three afternoons a week picking up after professional men who were nothing less than slobs. Maryanne had to resist the urge to write them each a note demanding that they put their dirty dishes in the sink and their soiled clothes in the laundry basket.

Rent-A-Maid had made housekeeping sound glamorous. It wasn't. In fact, it was the hardest, most physically exhausting job she'd ever undertaken.

By the end of the week, her nails were broken and chipped and her hands were red and chapped.

It was by chance rather than design that Maryanne bumped into Kramer late Friday afternoon. She was carrying a bag of groceries up the stairs when he bounded past her, taking the steps two at a time.

"Annie." He paused on the landing, waiting for her to catch up. "So how's it going?"

Maryanne didn't know what to say. She couldn't very well inform him that the highlight of her week was scraping a crusty patch off the bottom of an oven at one of the apartments she cleaned. She'd had such lofty expectations, such dreams. Nor could she casually announce that the stockbroker she cleaned for had spilled wine on his carpet and she'd spent an hour trying to get the stain out and broken two nails in the process.

"Fine," she lied. "Everything's just wonderful."

"Here, let me take that for you."

"Thanks." She handed him the single bag, her week's allotment of groceries. Unfortunately it was all she could afford. Everything had sounded so exciting when she started out; her plans had seemed so promising. The reality was proving to be something else again.

"Well, how do you like cleaning?"

"It's great, really great." It was amazing how easily the lie came. "I'm finding it . . . a challenge."

Kramer smiled absently. "I'm glad to hear it. Have you got your first paycheck yet?"

"I cashed it this afternoon." She'd spent more each week at the dry cleaners than she received in her first paycheck with Rent-A-Maid. The entire amount had gone for gas and food and there were only a few dollars left over. Her budget was tight, but she'd make it. She'd have to.

Kramer paused in front of her door and waited while she scrabbled through her purse, searching for the key.

"I hear you typing at night," she said. "Are you working on something special?"

"No."

She eyed him curiously. "How fast do you type? Eighty words a minute? A hundred? And for heaven's sake, why don't you use a computer like everyone else?"

"Sixty words a minute on a good day. And for your information, I happen to like my electric. It may be old, but it does the job."

She finally retrieved her key, conscious of his gaze on her hands.

Suddenly he grasped her fingers. "All right," he demanded. "What happened to you?"

CHAPTER FIVE

"NOTHING'S HAPPENED TO ME," Maryanne insisted hotly, pulling her hand free of Kramer's.

"Look at your nails," he said. "There isn't one that's not broken."

"You make it sound like I should be dragged before a firing squad at dawn. So I chipped a few nails this week. I'll survive." Although she was making light of it, each broken fingernail was like a small loss. She took pride in her perfect nails, or at least she had once.

His eyes narrowed as he scrutinized her. "There's something you're not telling me."

"I didn't realize you'd appointed yourself my father confessor."

Anger flashed in his dark eyes as he took the key from her unresisting fingers. He opened the door and, with one hand at her shoulder, urged her inside. "We need to talk."

"No, we don't." Maryanne marched into the apartment, plunked her bag of groceries on the kitchen counter and spun around to confront her neighbor. "Listen here, buster, you've made it perfectly clear that you don't want to have anything to do with me. That's your choice, and I'm certainly not going to bore you with the sorry details of my life."

He ignored her words and started pacing the small living area, pausing in front of the window. His presence filled the apartment, making it seem smaller than usual. He pivoted sharply, pointing an accusatory finger in her direction. "These broken nails came from swinging a dust mop around, did they? What the hell are you doing?"

Maryanne didn't answer him right away. She was angry, and his sudden concern for her welfare made her even angrier. "I told you before, I don't need a guardian."

"Against my advice, you took that stupid job. Anyone with half a brain would know it wasn't going to—"

"Will you stop acting like you're responsible for me?" Maryanne snapped.

"I can't help it. I *am* responsible for you. You wouldn't be here if I hadn't written that damn column. I don't want to intrude on your life any more than you want me to, but let's face it, there's no one else to look out for you. Sooner or later someone's going to take advantage of you."

That did it, Maryanne thought. She stalked over to him and jabbed her index finger into his chest with enough force to bend what remained of her nail. "In case you need reminding, I'm my own woman. I make my own decisions. I'll work any place I damn well please. Furthermore, I can take care of myself." She whirled around and opened her front door. "Now kindly leave!"

"No."

"No?" she repeated.

"No," he said again, returning to the window. He crossed his arms over his chest and sighed impatiently. "You haven't eaten, have you? I can tell, because you get testy when your stomach's empty."

"If you'd leave my apartment the way I asked that wouldn't be a problem."

"How about having dinner with me?"

The invitation took Maryanne by surprise. Her first impulse was to throw it back in his face. After an entire week of pretending she didn't exist, he had a lot of nerve even asking.

"Well?" he prompted.

"Where?" As if that made a difference. Maryanne was famished, and the thought of sharing her meal with Kramer was more tempting than she wanted to admit, even to herself.

"The diner."

"Are you going to order chili?"

"Are you going to ask them to remove the bean sprouts from your sandwich?"

Maryanne hesitated. She felt confused by all her contradictory emotions. She was strongly attracted to Kramer and she admired his talent. Every time they were together she caught herself hoping they could become friends—more than friends. But, equally often, he infuriated her or left her feeling depressed. He made the most outlandish remarks to her. He seemed to have appointed himself her legal guardian. When he wasn't issuing decrees, he neglected her as if she were nothing more than a nuisance. And to provide a finishing touch, she was lying to her parents because of him! Well, maybe that wasn't quite fair, but...

"I'll throw in dessert," he coaxed with a smile.

The smile was her Waterloo, yet she still struggled. "A la mode?"

His grin widened. "You drive a hard bargain."

Maryanne's eyes met his and although Kramer could make her angrier than anyone she'd ever known, a smile trembled on her own lips.

They agreed to meet a half hour later. That gave Maryanne time to unpack her groceries, change clothes and freshen her makeup. She found herself humming as she applied lip gloss, wondering if she was reading too much significance into this impromptu dinner date.

When Kramer came to her door to pick her up, Maryanne noted that he'd changed out of his suit and into jeans and a fisherman's sweater. It was the first time she'd seen him without the raincoat, other than the day he'd played basketball with the neighborhood boys. He looked good. All right, she admitted grudgingly, he looked fantastic.

"You dressed up," she said before she could stop herself, grateful at least that she'd understated her attraction to him.

"So did you. You look nice."

"Thanks."

"Before I forget to tell you, word has it the elevator's going to be fixed Monday morning."

"Really? That's the best news I've heard all week." Goodness, could she take all these glad tidings at once? First Kramer had actually invited her out on a date, and now she wouldn't have to hike four flights of stairs every afternoon. Life was indeed treating her well.

They were several blocks from the apartment building before Maryanne realized Kramer was driving in the opposite direction of the diner. She said as much.

"Do you like Chinese food?" he asked.

"I love it."

"The diner's short-staffed—one of the waitresses quit. I thought Chinese food might be interesting, and I promise we won't have to wait for a table."

It sounded heavenly to Maryanne. She didn't know how significant Kramer's decision to take her to a different restaurant might be. Perhaps it was foolish, but Maryanne hoped it meant she was becoming special to him. As if guessing her thoughts, Kramer was unusually quiet on the drive into Seattle's International District.

So much for romance. Maryanne could almost hear his thoughts. If she were a betting woman, she'd place odds on the way their dinner conversation would go. First Kramer would try to find out exactly what tasks had been assigned to her by Rent-A-Maid. Then he'd try to convince her to quit.

Only she wasn't going to let him. She was her own woman, and she'd said it often enough to convince herself. If this newsman thought he could sway her with a fancy dinner and a few well-spoken words, then he was about to learn a valuable lesson.

The restaurant proved to be a Chinese version of the greasy spoon where Kramer ate regularly. The minute they walked into the compact room, Maryanne's senses were greeted with a wide variety of tantalizing scents. Pungent spices and oils wafted through the air, and the smells were so appealing it was all Maryanne could do not to follow them into the kitchen. She knew before sampling a single bite that the food would be some of the best Oriental cuisine she'd ever tasted.

An elderly Chinese gentleman greeted Kramer as if he were a long-lost relative. The two shared a brief exchange in Chinese before the man escorted them to a table. He shouted into the kitchen, and a brightly painted ceramic pot of tea was quickly delivered to their table.

Kramer and Maryanne were never given menus. Almost from the moment they were seated, food began appearing on their table. An appetizer plate came first, with several items Maryanne couldn't readily identify. But she was too hungry to care. Everything was delicious and she happily devoured one after another.

"You seem well acquainted with the waiter," Maryanne commented, once the appetizer plate was empty. She barely had time to catch her breath before a bowl of thick spicy soup was brought to them by the same elderly gentleman. He paused and smiled proudly at Kramer, then glanced at Maryanne, before nodding in a profound way.

"Wong Su's the owner. I went to school with his son."

"Is that where you picked up Chinese?"

"Yes. I only know a few words, just enough to get the gist of what he's saying," he answered brusquely, reaching for his spoon.

"What was it he said when we first came in? I noticed you seemed quick to disagree with him."

Kramer dipped his spoon into the soup, ignoring her question.

"Kramer?"

"He said you're too thin."

Maryanne shook her head, knowing immediately that he was lying. "If he really thought that, you'd have agreed with him."

"All right, all right," Kramer muttered, looking severely displeased. "I should have known better than to bring a woman to Wong Su's place. He immediately assumed there was something romantic between us. He said you'd give me many fine sons."

"How sweet."

Her words instantly captured Kramer's attention. He dropped his spoon beside the bowl with a clatter, planted his elbows on the table and glared at her heatedly. "Now don't go all sentimental on me. There's nothing between us and there never will be."

Maryanne promptly saluted. "Aye, aye, Captain," she mocked.

"Good. Well, now that's settled, tell me about your week."

"Tell me about yours," she countered, unwilling to change the subject to herself quite so easily. "You seemed a whole lot busier than I was."

"I went to work, came home..."

"...worked some more," she finished for him. Another plate, heaped high with sizzling hot chicken and crisp vegetables was brought by Wong Su, who offered Maryanne a toothy grin.

Kramer frowned at his friend and said something in Chinese that caused the older man to laugh outright. When Kramer returned his attention to Maryanne, he was scowling again. "For heaven's sake, don't encourage him."

"What did I do?" To the best of her knowledge she was innocent of any wrongdoing.

Kramer thought it over for a moment. "Never mind, it won't do any good to tell you."

Other steaming dishes arrived—prawns with cashew nuts, then ginger beef and barbecued pork, each accompanied by small bowls of rice until virtually every inch of the small table was covered.

"You were telling me about your week," Maryanne reminded him, reaching for the dish in the center of the crowded table.

"No, I wasn't," Kramer retorted.

With a scornful sigh, Maryanne passed Kramer the chicken. "All right, have it your way."

"You're going to needle me to death until you find out what I'm working on in my spare time, aren't you?"

"Of course not." If he didn't want her to know, then fine, she had no intention of asking again. Acting as nonchalant as possible, she helped herself to a thick slice of the pork. She dipped it into a small dish of hot mustard, which proved to be a bit more potent than she'd expected; her eyes rapidly started to water.

Mumbling under his breath, Kramer handed her his napkin. "Here."

"I'm all right." She wiped the moisture from her eyes and blinked a couple of times before reaching for her water glass. Once she'd composed herself, she returned to the subject at hand. "On the contrary, Mr. Adams, whatever project so intensely occupies your time is your own concern."

"Spoken like a true aristocrat."

"Obviously you don't care to share it with me."

He gave an exaggerated sigh. "It's a novel," he said. "There now, are you satisfied?"

"A novel," she repeated coolly. "Really. And all along, I thought you were taking in typing jobs on the side."

He glared at her, but the edges of his mouth turned up in a reluctant grin. "I don't want to talk about the plot, all right? I'm afraid that would water it down."

"I understand perfectly."

"Damn it all, Annie, would you stop looking at me with those big blue eyes of yours? I already feel guilty as hell without you smiling serenely at me and trying to act so blasé."

"Guilty about what?"

He expelled his breath sharply. "Listen," he said in a low voice, leaning toward her. "As much as I hate to admit this, you're right. It's none of my business where you work or how many nails you break or how much you're paid. But damn it all, I'm worried about you."

She raised her chopsticks in an effort to stop him. "It seems to me I've heard this argument before. Actually, it's downright boring hearing it over and over again."

Kramer dropped his voice even lower. "You've been sheltered all your life. I know you don't want me to feel responsible for what you're doing—or for you. And I wish I didn't. Unfortunately I can't help it. Believe me, I've tried. It doesn't work. Every night I lie awake wondering what trouble you're going to get into next. I don't know what's going to happen first—you working yourself to death, or me getting an ulcer."

Maryanne's gaze fell to her hands, and the uneven length of her once perfectly uniform fingernails. "They are rather pitiful, aren't they?"

Kramer glanced at them and grimaced. "As a personal favor to me would you consider giving up the job at Rent-A-Maid?" He ran his fingers through his hair, sighing heavily. "It doesn't come easy to ask you this, Annie. If for no other reason, do it because you owe me a favor for finding you the apartment. But for heaven's sake, quit that job."

She didn't answer him right away. She wanted to do as he asked, because she was falling in love with him. Because she craved his approval. Yet she wanted to reject his entreaties, flout his demands. Because he made her feel confused and contrary and full of unpredictable emotions.

"If it'll do any good, I'll promise not to interfere again," he said, his voice so quiet it was almost a whisper.

"As a personal favor to you," she repeated, nodding slowly. So much for refusing to be swayed by dinner and a few well-chosen words.

Their eyes met and held for a long moment. Deliberately, as though going against every dictate of his will, Kramer reached out and brushed an auburn curl from her cheek. His touch was light yet strangely intimate, as intimate as a kiss. His fingers lingered on her cheek and it was all Maryanne could do not to cover his hand with her own and close her eyes to savor the wealth of sensations that settled around her.

Kramer's dark eyes narrowed, and she could tell he was struggling. She could read it in every line, every feature of his handsome face, but against what, she could only speculate. He didn't want to be attracted to her; that much was obvious.

As if needing to break contact with her eyes, he lowered his gaze to her mouth. Whether it was intentional or not, Maryanne didn't know, his thumb inched closer to her lips, easing toward the corner. Then, with an abrupt movement, he pulled his hand away and returned to his meal, eating quickly and methodically.

Maryanne tried to eat, but her own appetite was gone. Wong Su refused payment although Kramer tried to insist. Instead the elderly man said something in Chinese that sent every eye in the place straight to Maryanne. She smiled benignly, wondering what he could possibly have said that would make the great Kramer Adams blush.

The drive back to the apartment was as silent as the one to the restaurant had been. Maryanne considered asking Kramer exactly what Wong Su had said just before they'd left, but she thought better of it.

By unspoken agreement, they took their time walking up the four flights of stairs. "Will you come in for coffee?" Maryanne asked when they arrived at her door.

"I can't tonight," Kramer said after several all-too-quiet moments.

"I don't bite, you know." His eyes didn't waver from hers. The attraction was there—she could feel it as surely as she had his touch at dinner.

"I'd like to finish my chapter."

So he was going to close her out once again, erect that wall higher. "Don't work too hard," she said, opening the apartment door. Her disappointment was keen, but she managed to disguise it behind a shrug. "Thank you for dinner. It was delicious."

Kramer thrust his hands into his pockets. It might have been her imagination, but she thought he did it to keep from reaching for her. The idea comforted her ego and she smiled up at him warmly.

She was about to close the door when he stopped her. "Yes?" she asked.

His eyes were as piercing and dark as she'd ever seen them. "My typing. Does it keep you awake nights?"

"No," she told him and shook her head for emphasis. "The book must be going well."

He nodded, then sighed. "Listen, would it be possible..." He paused and started again. "Are you busy tomorrow night? I've got two tickets to the Seattle Repertory Theater and I was wondering . . ."

"I'd love to go," she said eagerly, before he'd even finished the question.

Judging by the expression on his face, the invitation seemed to be as much a surprise to him as it was to her. "I'll see you tomorrow then."

"Right," she answered brightly. "Tomorrow."

THE AFTERNOON was glorious, with just the right mixture of wind and sunshine. Hands clasped behind her back, Maryanne strolled across the grass of Volunteer Park, kicking up leaves as she went. She'd spent the morning researching an article she hoped to sell to a local magazine and she was taking a break.

The basketball court was occupied by several teenage boys, a couple of whom she recognized from the day she'd moved. With time on her hands and an afternoon to enjoy, Maryanne paused to watch the hotly contested game. Sitting on a picnic table, she swung her legs, content to laze away the sunny afternoon. Everything was going so well. Without hardly any difficulty she'd found another job. Kramer probably wasn't going to approve of this one, either, but that was just too bad.

"Hi." A girl of about thirteen, wearing a jean jacket and tight black stretch pants, strolled up to the picnic table. "You're Mr. Adams's girlfriend, aren't you?"

Maryanne would have liked to think so, but she knew better. "What makes you ask that?"

"You moved in with him, didn't you?"

"Not exactly. I live in the apartment next door."

"I didn't believe Eddie when he said Mr. Adams had a woman. He's never had anyone live with him before. He's just not the type, if you know what I mean."

Maryanne did know. She was learning not to take his attitude toward her personally. The better acquainted she became with Kramer, the more clearly she realized that he considered all women a nuisance. The first night they met, he'd mentioned that he'd been in love once, but his tone had been so casual it implied this romance was merely a long-ago mistake. He'd talked about the experience as if it meant little or nothing to him. Maryanne wasn't sure she believed that.

"Mr. Adams is a really neat guy. All the kids like him a lot." The girl smiled, suggesting she was one of his legion of admirers. "I'm Gloria Masterson."

Maryanne held out her hand. "Maryanne Simpson."

Gloria smiled shyly. "If you're not his woman, are you . . . you know, his sweetheart?"

"Not really. We're just friends."

"That's what he said when I asked him about you."

"Oh." It wasn't as though she could expect him to admit anything more.

"Mr. Adams comes around every now and again and talks to us kids in the park. I think he's checking up on us and making sure no one's into drugs or gangs."

Maryanne smiled. That sounded exactly like something Kramer would do.

"Only a few kids around here are that stupid, but you know, I think a couple of the boys might have been tempted to try something if it weren't for Mr. Adams."

"Hey, Gloria." A lanky youth from the basketball court called out. "Come here, woman."

Gloria sighed loudly, then shouted. "Just a minute." She turned back to Maryanne. "I'm really not Eddie's woman. He just likes to think so."

Maryanne smiled. She wished she could say the same thing about her and Kramer. "It was nice to meet you, Gloria. Maybe I'll see you around."

"That'd be great."

"Gloria," Eddie shouted, "are you coming or not?"

The teenage girl shook her head. "I don't know why I put up with him."

Maryanne left the park soon afterward. The first thing she noticed when she got home was an envelope taped to her door.

She waited until she was inside the apartment to open it, and as she did a single ticket and a note slipped out. "I got stuck at the office," the note read. "The curtain goes up at eight—don't be late. K."

Maryanne was mildly disappointed that Kramer wouldn't be driving her to the play, but she decided to splurge and take a taxi. By seven-thirty, when the cab arrived, she was dressed and ready. She wore her best evening attire, a long black velvet skirt and matching blazer with a cream-colored silk blouse. She'd even put on her pearl earrings and cameo necklace.

The theater was one of the nicest in town, and Maryanne's heart sang with excitement as the usher escorted her to her seat. Kramer hadn't arrived yet and she looked around expectantly.

The curtain was about to go up when a man she mentally categorized as wealthy and a bit of a charmer settled in the vacant seat next to hers.

"Excuse me," he said, leaning toward her, smiling warmly. "I'm Griff Bradly. Kramer Adams sent me."

It didn't take Maryanne two seconds to figure out what Kramer had done. The low-down rat had matched her up with someone he considered more appropriate. Someone he assumed she had more in common with.

Someone wealthy and slick. Someone her father would approve of.

"Where's Kramer?" Maryanne demanded. She bolted to her feet and grabbed her purse, jerking it so hard the tiny gold chain strap threatened to break.

Griff looked taken aback by her sharp question. "You mean he didn't discuss this evening with you?"

"He invited me to this play. I assumed . . . I believed the two of us would be attending it together. He didn't say a word about you. I'm sorry, but I can't agree to this arrangement." She started to edge her way out of the row just as the curtain rose.

To her dismay, Griff followed her into the aisle. "I'm sure there's been some misunderstanding."

"You bet there has," Maryanne said, loudly enough to attract the angry glares of several patrons sitting in the aisle seats. She rushed toward the exit with Griff in hot pursuit.

"If you'll give me a moment to explain—"

"It won't be necessary."

"You are Maryanne Simpson of the New York Simpsons?"

"Yes," she said, walking directly outside. Standing on the curb she raised her hand and shouted, "Taxi!"

Griff raced around to stand in front of her. "Surely there isn't any need to rush off like this. Kramer was doing me a good turn."

"And me a rotten one. Listen, Mr. Bradly, you look like a very nice gentleman, and under any other circumstances I would have been more than happy to make your acquaintance, but there's been a terrible misunderstanding."

"But—"

"I'm sorry, I really am." A cab raced toward her and squealed to a halt.

Griff opened the back door for her, looking more charming and debonair than ever. "I don't know that my heart will recover. You're really quite lovely, you know."

Maryanne sighed. The man was overdoing it, but he certainly didn't deserve the treatment she was giving him. She smiled and apologized again, then swiftly turned her attention to the driver and recited her address.

Maryanne fumed during the entire ride back to her apartment. Rarely had she been more furious. If Kramer Adams thought he could play matchmaker with her, he was about to learn that everything he'd ever heard about redheads was true.

"Hey, lady, are you all right?" the cabbie asked.

"I'm fine," she said stiffly.

"That guy you were with back at the theater didn't try anything, did he?"

"No, some other man did, only he's not going to get away with it." The driver pulled into her street. "That's the building there," Maryanne told him. She reached into her purse for her wallet and pulled out some of her precious cash, including a generous tip. Then she ran into the apartment building, heedless of her clothes or her high-heeled shoes.

For the first time since moving in, Maryanne didn't pause to rest on the third-floor landing. Her anger carried her all the way to Kramer's apartment door. She could hear him typing inside, and the sound added to her temper. Dragging breath through her lungs, she slammed her fist against the door.

"Hold on a minute," she heard him grumble.

His shocked look as he threw open the door would have been comical in different circumstances. "Maryanne, what are you doing here?"

"That was a rotten underhanded thing to do, you deceiving, conniving, low-down . . . rat!"

Kramer did an admirable job of composing himself. He buried his hands in his pockets and smiled nonchalantly. "I take it you and Griff Bradly didn't hit it off?"

CHAPTER SIX

MARYANNE WAS SO FURIOUS she couldn't find the words to express her outrage. She opened and closed her mouth twice before she collected herself enough to proceed.

"I told you before that I didn't want you interfering in my life, and I meant it."

"I was doing you a favor," Kramer countered, clearly unmoved by her angry display. In fact, he yawned loudly, covering his mouth with the back of his hand. "Griff's a stockbroker friend of mine and one hell of a nice guy. If you'd given him half a chance, you might have found that out yourself. I could see the two of you becoming good friends. Why don't you give it a try? You two might hit it off."

"The only thing I'd consider hitting is *you*." To her horror, tears of rage flooded her eyes. "Don't ever try that again. Do you understand?" Not waiting for his reply, she turned abruptly, stalked down the hall to her apartment and unlocked the door. She flung it shut with sufficient force to rattle the windows on three floors.

She paced back and forth several times, blew her nose once and decided she hadn't told him nearly enough. Throwing open her door, she rushed down the hall to Kramer's apartment again. She banged twice as hard as she had originally.

Kramer opened the door, wearing a martyr's expression. He cocked one eyebrow expressively. "What is it this time?"

"And furthermore you're the biggest coward I've ever met. If I still worked for the newspaper, I'd write a column so all Seattle would know exactly what kind of man you really are." Her voice wobbled just a little, but that didn't diminish the strength of her indignation.

She stomped back to her own apartment and she hadn't been there two seconds before there was a pounding on her door. It didn't surprise her to find Kramer Adams on the other side. He might have appeared calm, but his eyes sparked with an angry fire. They narrowed slightly as he glowered at her.

"What did you just say?" he asked.

"You heard me. You're nothing but a coward. Coward, coward, coward!" With that she slammed her door so hard that a framed family photo hanging on the wall crashed to the floor. Luckily the glass didn't break.

Her chest heaving, Maryanne picked up the photo, wiped it off and carefully replaced it. But for all her outward composure, her hands were trembling. No sooner had she completed the task when Kramer beat on her door a second time.

"Now what?" she demanded whipping open the door. "I would have thought you got my message."

"I got it all right. I just don't happen to like it."

"Tough." She would have slammed the door again, but before she could act, a loud banging came from the direction of the floor. Not knowing what it was, Maryanne instinctively jumped back.

Kramer drew a deep breath, and Maryanne could tell he was making an effort to compose himself. "All right,

Mrs. McBride," Kramer shouted at the floor, "we'll hold it down."

"Who's Mrs. McBride?"

"The lady who lives in the apartment below you."

"Oh." Maryanne had been too infuriated to realize she was shouting loudly enough for half the apartment building to hear. She felt ashamed at her loss of control and guilty for disturbing her neighbors—but she was still furious with Kramer.

The man in question glared at her. "Do you think it's possible to discuss this situation without involving any more doors?" he asked sharply. "Or would you rather wait until someone phones the police and we're both arrested for disturbing the peace?"

She glared back at him defiantly. "Very funny," she said, turning around and walking into her apartment. As she knew he would, Kramer followed her inside.

Maryanne moved into the kitchen. Preparing a pot of coffee gave her a few extra minutes to gather her dignity, which had been as abused as her apartment door. Mixed with the anger was a chilling pain that cut straight through her heart. Kramer's thinking so little of her that he could casually pass her on to another man was mortifying enough. But knowing he considered it a favor only heaped on the humiliation.

"Annie, please listen—"

"Did it ever occur to you that arranging this date with Griff might offend me?" she cried.

Kramer seemed reluctant to answer. "Yes," he finally said, "it did. I tried to catch you earlier this afternoon, but you weren't in. This wasn't the kind of situation I felt comfortable explaining in a note, so I took the easy way out and left Griff to introduce himself. I didn't realize you'd take it so personally."

"How else was I supposed to take it?"

Kramer glanced away uncomfortably. "Let's just say I was hoping you'd meet him and the two of you would spend the evening getting to know each other. Griff comes from a well-established family and—"

"That's supposed to impress me?"

"He's the type of man your father would arrange for you to meet," Kramer said, his voice sandpaper-gruff.

"How many times do I have to tell you I don't need a second father?" His mention of her family reminded her of the way she was deceiving them, which brought a powerful sense of remorse.

He muttered tersely under his breath, then shook his head. "Obviously I blew it. Would it help if I apologized?"

An apology, even a sincere one, wouldn't soon dissolve the hurt that had become wrapped around her heart. She looked up, about to tell him exactly that when her eyes forcefully locked with his.

He stood a safe distance from her, his expression so tender that her battered heart rolled defenselessly to her feet. She knew she ought to throw him out of her home and refuse to ever speak to him again. No one would blame her. She tried to rally her anger, but something she couldn't explain or understand stopped her.

All the emotion must have sharpened her perceptions. Never had she been more aware of Kramer as a man. The moment felt full; the space separating them seemed to close, drawing them toward each other. She could smell the clean scent of the soap he used and hear the music of the rain as it danced against her window. She hadn't even realized, until this moment, that it was raining.

"I am sorry," he said quietly.

Maryanne nodded and wiped the moisture from her eyes. She wasn't a woman who cried easily, and the tears were a surprise.

"What you said about my being a coward is true," Kramer admitted. He sighed heavily. "You frighten me, Annie."

"You mean my temper?"

"No, I deserved that." He grinned that lazy insolent grin of his.

"What is it about me you find so unappealing?" She had to know what it was that was driving him away, no matter how much the truth damaged her pride.

"Unappealing?" His abrupt laugh was filled with irony. "I wish I could find something, *anything*, unappealing about you, but I can't." Dropping his gaze, he stepped back and cleared his throat. When he spoke again, his words were brusque, impatient. "I was a lot more comfortable with you before we met."

"You thought of me as a debutante."

"I assumed you were a pampered immature...girl. Not a woman. I expected to find you ambitious and selfish, so eager to impress your father with what you could do that it didn't matter how many people you walked over. Then we did the Celebrity Debate, and I realized none of the things I wanted to believe about you were true."

"Then why—"

"The thing you've got to understand," Kramer added forcefully, "is that I don't want to become involved with you."

"That message has come through loud and clear." She moistened her lips and cast her gaze toward the floor, afraid he'd see how vulnerable he made her feel.

Suddenly he was standing directly in front of her, so close his breath warmed her face. With one gentle finger, he lifted her chin, raising her eyes to his.

"All evening I was telling myself how noble I was," he said. "Griff Bradly is far better suited to you than I'll ever be."

"Stop saying that!"

He wrapped his arms around her waist and pulled her close. "There can't ever be anything between us," he said, his voice rough. "I learned my lesson years ago, and I'm not going to repeat that mistake." But contrary to everything he was saying, his mouth lowered to hers until their lips touched. The kiss was slow and familiar. Their bottom lips clung as Kramer eased away from her.

"That wasn't supposed to happen," he murmured.

"I won't tell anyone if you won't," she whispered.

"Just remember what I said," he whispered back. "I don't do well with rich girls. I already found that out. The hard way."

"I'll remember," she said softly, looking up at him.

"Good." And then he kissed her again.

IT WAS THREE DAYS before Maryanne saw Kramer. She didn't need anyone to tell her he was avoiding her. Again. Maybe he thought falling in love would wreak havoc with his comfortable well-ordered life. If he'd given her a chance, Maryanne would have told Kramer she didn't expect him to fill her days. She had her new job, and she was fixing up her apartment. Most important, she had her writing, which kept her busy the rest of the time. She'd recently queried a magazine about doing a humorous article on her experiences working for Rent-A-Maid.

"Here's Kramer now," Barbara whispered as she hurried past Maryanne, balancing three plates.

Automatically Maryanne reached for a water glass and a menu and followed Kramer to the booth. He was halfway into his seat when he saw her. He froze and his narrowed accusing gaze flew across the room to the middle-aged waitress.

Barbara didn't appear in the least intimidated. "Hey, what did you expect?" she called out. "We were one girl short, and when Maryanne applied for the job she gave you as a reference. Besides, she's a good worker."

Kramer didn't bother to look at the menu. Standing beside the table, Maryanne reached for her green order pad.

"I'll have the chili," he ordered gruffly.

"With or without cheese?"

"Without," he bellowed, then quickly lowered his voice. "How long have you been working here?"

"Since Monday morning. Don't look so angry. You were the one who told me about the job. Remember?"

"I don't want you working here!"

"Why not? It's a respectable establishment. Honestly, Kramer, what did you expect me to do? I had to find another job, and fast. I can't expect to sell any articles for at least a month, if then. I've got to find some way of paying the bills."

"You could have done a hell of a lot better than Mom's Place if you wanted to be a waitress."

"Are we going to argue? Again?" she asked with an impatient sigh.

"No," he answered, grabbing his napkin just in time to catch a violent sneeze.

Now that she had a chance to study him, she saw his nose was red and his eyes rheumy. In fact he looked downright miserable. "You've got a cold."

"Are you always this brilliant?"

"I try to be. And I'll try to ignore your rudeness. Would you like a glass of orange juice or a couple of aspirin?"

"No, Florence Nightingale, all I want is my usual bowl of chili, *without* the cheese. Have you got that?"

"Yes, of course," she said, writing it down. Kramer certainly seemed to be in a rotten mood, but that was nothing new. Maryanne seemed to bring out the worst in him.

Barbara met her at the counter. "From the looks your boyfriend's been sending me, he'd gladly cut off my head. What's with him, anyway?"

"I don't think he's feeling well," Maryanne answered in a low worried voice.

"Men, especially sick ones, are the biggest babies that ever walked the earth," Barbara said wryly. "They get a little virus and think someone should rush in to tape a documentary on their life-threatening condition. My advice to you is let him wallow in his misery all by himself."

"But he looks like he might have a fever," Maryanne whispered.

"And he isn't old enough to take an aspirin all on his own?" The older woman glanced behind her. "His order's up. You want me to take it to him?"

"No..."

"Don't worry, if he gets smart with me I'll just whack him alongside the head. Someone needs to put that man in his place."

Maryanne reached for the large bowl of chili. "I'll do it."

"Yes," Barbara said, grinning broadly. "I have a feeling you will."

MARYANNE ARRIVED HOME several hours later. Her feet hurt and her back ached, but she felt a pleasant glow of satisfaction. After three days of waitressing, she was beginning to get the knack of keeping orders straight and remembering everything she needed to do. It wasn't the job of her dreams, but she was making a living wage, certainly better money than she'd been getting from Rent-A-Maid. Not only that, the tips were good. Maryanne didn't dare imagine what her family would say if they found out, though. She suffered a stab of remorse every time she thought about the way she was deceiving them. In fact, it was simpler not to think about it at all.

After his initial reaction, Kramer hadn't so much as mentioned her working at Mom's Place. He clearly wasn't thrilled, but that didn't surprise her. Little, if anything, she'd done from the moment she'd met him had gained his approval.

Maryanne had grown accustomed to falling asleep most nights to the sound of Kramer's typing. She found herself listening for it when she climbed into bed. But she didn't hear it that night or the two nights that followed.

"How's Kramer?" Barbara asked her on Friday afternoon.

"I don't know." Maryanne hadn't seen him in days, but then, she rarely did.

"He must have got a really bad bug."

Maryanne hated the way her heart reacted. She'd tried not to think about him. Not that she'd been successful...

"His column hasn't been in the paper all week. The *Sun*'s been running some of his old ones—Kramer's Classics. Did you read the one last night?" Barbara asked, laughing. "He said it was a good thing the United States wasn't around when Moses was negotiating with the Egyptians. Can't you picture it? We'd get all involved in the meditations, wanting to do whatever we could to keep everything nice and friendly."

As a matter of fact, Maryanne had read the piece and been highly amused. As always she'd been impressed with Kramer's dry wit. They often disagreed—Kramer was too much of a pessimist to suit her—but she couldn't help admiring his skill with words.

Since the afternoon he'd found her at Mom's, Kramer hadn't eaten there again. Maryanne didn't consider that so strange. He went to great lengths to ensure they didn't run into each other. She did feel mildly guilty that he'd decided to stay away from his favorite diner, but it *was* his choice, after all.

During the rest of her shift, Maryanne had to struggle to keep Kramer out of her mind. His apartment had been unusually quiet for the past few days, but she hadn't been concerned about it. Now she was.

"Do you think he's all right?" she asked Barbara some time later.

"He's a big boy," the older woman was quick to remind her. "He can take care of himself."

Maryanne wasn't so sure. After work, she hurried home, convinced she'd find Kramer hovering near death, too ill to call for help. She didn't even stop at her own apartment, but went directly to his.

She knocked politely, anticipating all kinds of disasters when there was no response.

"Kramer?" She pounded on his door and yelled his name, battling down a rising sense of panic. She envisioned him lying on his bed, suffering—or worse. "Kramer, please answer the door," she pleaded, wondering if there was someone in the building with a passkey.

She'd waited hours, it seemed, before he yanked open the door.

"Are you all right?" she demanded, so relieved to see him she could hardly keep from hurling herself into his arms. Relieved, that is, until she got a good look at him.

"I was feeling just great," he told her gruffly, "until I had to get out of bed to answer the stupid door. Which, incidentally, woke me up."

Maryanne pressed her fingers over her mouth to hide her hysterical laughter. If Kramer felt anywhere near as bad as he looked, then she should seriously consider phoning for an ambulance. He wore gray sweatpants and a faded plaid robe, one she would guess had been moth fodder for years. His choice of clothes was the least of her concerns, however. He resembled someone who'd just surfaced from a four-day drunk. His eyes were red and his face ashen. He scowled at her and it was clear the moment he spoke that his disposition was as cheery as his appearance.

"I take it there's a reason for this uninvited visit?" he growled, then sneezed fiercely.

"Yes..." Maryanne hedged, not knowing exactly what to do now. "I just wanted to make sure you're all right."

"Okay, you've seen me. I'm going to live, so you can leave in good conscience." He would have closed the door, but Maryanne stepped forward and boldly edged her way into his apartment.

In the weeks they'd lived next door to each other, she'd never once seen his home. The muted earth colors, the rich leather furniture and polished wood floors appealed to her immediately. Despite her worry about his condition, she smiled; this room reminded her of Kramer, with papers and books littering every available space. His apartment seemed at least twice the size of hers. He'd once mentioned that it was larger, but after becoming accustomed to her own small rooms, this spaciousness of his was a pleasant shock.

"In case you haven't noticed, I'm in no mood for company," he informed her in a surly voice.

"Have you been to a doctor?"

"No."

"Do you need anything?"

"Peace and quiet," he muttered.

"You could have bronchitis or pneumonia or something."

"I'm perfectly fine. At least, I was until you arrived." He walked across the carpet—a dark green-and-gold Persian, Maryanne noted automatically—and slumped onto an overstuffed sofa piled with blankets and pillows. The television was on, its volume turned very low.

"Then why haven't you been to work?"

"I'm on vacation."

"Personally, I would have chosen a tropical island over a sofa in my own apartment." She advanced purposefully into his kitchen and stopped short when she caught sight of the dirty dishes stacked a foot high in the stainless-steel sink. She was amazed he could cram so much into such a tight space.

"This place is a mess!" she declared, hands on her hips.

"Go ahead and call the health department if you're so concerned."

"I probably should." Instead, she walked straight to the sink, rolled up her sleeves and started stacking the dishes on the counter.

"What are you doing now?" Kramer shouted from the living room.

"Cleaning up."

He muttered something she couldn't hear, which was probably for the best.

"Go lie down, Kramer," she instructed. "When I'm done here, I'll heat you some soup. You've got to get your strength back in order to suffer properly."

At first he let that comment pass. Then, as if she was taxing him to the limit of his endurance, he called out, "The way you care is truly touching."

"I was hoping you'd notice." For someone who'd been outraged at the sight of her dishpan hands a week earlier, he seemed oddly unconcerned that she was washing his dirty dishes. Not that Maryanne minded. It made her feel good to be doing something for him.

She soon found herself humming as she rinsed off the dishes and set them in his dishwasher.

Fifteen minutes passed without their exchanging a word. When Maryanne had finished, she looked in the living room and wasn't surprised to find him sound asleep on the sofa. A curious feeling tugged at her heart as she gazed down at him. He lay on his back with his left hand flung across his forehead. His features were relaxed, but there was nothing remotely angelic about him. Not about the way his thick dark lashes brushed the arch of his cheek—or about the slow hoarse breaths that whispered through his half-open mouth.

Maryanne felt a strong urge to brush the hair from his forehead, to touch him, but she resisted. She was afraid he'd wake up. And she was even more afraid she wouldn't want to stop touching him.

Moving about the living room, she turned off the television, picked up things here and there and straightened a few piles of magazines. She should leave now; she knew that. Kramer wouldn't welcome her staying. She eyed the door regretfully, looking for an excuse to linger. She closed her eyes and listened to the sound of Kramer's raspy breathing.

More by chance than design, Maryanne found herself standing next to his typewriter. Feeling brave, and more than a little foolish, she dropped her gaze to the stack of paper resting beside it. Glancing over her shoulder to make sure he was still asleep, Maryanne carefully turned over the top page and quickly read the last couple of paragraphs on page 212. The story wasn't finished, but she could tell he'd stopped during a cliffhanger scene.

Kramer had been so secretive about his project that she dared not invade his privacy any more than she already had. She neatly turned the single sheet back over, taking care to place it exactly as she'd found it.

Once again, she reminded herself that she should go back to her own apartment, but she felt strangely reluctant to end these moments with Kramer. Even a sleeping Kramer who would certainly be cranky when he woke up.

Seeking some way to occupy herself, she moved down the hall and into the bathroom, picking up several soiled towels on the way. His bed was unmade. She would have been surprised to find it in any other condition. The sheets and blankets were sagging against the floor, and two or three sets of clothing were scattered in all directions.

Without questioning the wisdom of her actions, she bundled up the dirty laundry to take to the coin-operated machine in the basement. She loaded it into a large garbage bag, then set about vigorously cleaning the apartment. Scrubbing, scouring and sweeping were skills she'd perfected in her Rent-A-Maid days. If nothing else, she'd had lots of practice cleaning up after messy bachelors.

Studying the contents of his refrigerator, more than an hour later, proved to be a humorous adventure. She found an unopened bottle of wine, a carton of broken egg shells and one limp strand of celery. Concocting anything edible from that would be impossible, so she searched the apartment until she found his keys. Then, with his garbage bag full of laundry in her arms, she let herself out the door, closing it softly.

She returned a half hour later, clutching two bags of groceries bought with her tip money. To her delight, Kramer was still asleep. She smiled down at him indulgently before she began preparing his dinner.

She was in the kitchen peeling potatoes when she heard Kramer get up. She continued her task, knowing he'd discover she was there soon enough. He stopped cold when he did.

"What are you doing here?"

"Cooking your dinner."

"I'm not hungry," he snapped with no evidence of appreciation for her efforts.

His eyes widened as he glanced around. "Good Lord, you've cleaned the place."

"I didn't think you'd notice," she answered sweetly, popping a small piece of raw potato in her mouth. "I'll get soup to the boiling stage before I leave you to your...peace of mind. It should only take another ten or fifteen minutes. Can you endure me that much longer?"

He made another of his typical grumbling replies before disappearing. No more than two seconds had passed before he let out a bellow loud enough to shake the roof tiles.

"What did you do to my bed?" he demanded as he stormed into the kitchen.

"I made it."

"What else have you been up to? Dammit, a man isn't safe in his own home with you around."

"Don't look so put out, Kramer. All I did was straighten up the place a bit. It was a mess."

"I happen to like messes. I thrive in messes. The last thing I want or need is some neat-freak invading my home, organizing my life."

"Don't exaggerate," Maryanne said serenely, as she added a pile of diced carrots to the simmering broth. "All I did was pick up a few things here and there and run a load of laundry."

"You did my laundry, too?" he exploded, running both hands through his hair. Heaven only knew, she thought, what would happen if he learned she'd read a single word of his precious manuscript.

"Everything's been folded and put away, so you needn't worry."

Kramer abruptly left the kitchen, only to return a couple of moments later. He circled the table slowly and precisely, then took several deep breaths.

"Listen, Annie," he began carefully, "it isn't that I don't appreciate what you've done, but I don't need a nurse. Or a housekeeper."

She looked up, meeting his eyes, her own large and guileless. "I quite agree," she answered.

"You do?" Some of the stiffness left his shoulders. "Then you aren't going to take offense?"

"No, why should I?"

"No reason," he answered, eyeing her suspiciously.

"I was thinking that what you really need," she said, smiling at him gently, "is a wife."

CHAPTER SEVEN

"A WIFE," KRAMER ECHOED. His dark eyes widened in undisguised horror. It was as if Maryanne had suggested he climb to the top of the apartment building and leap off.

"Don't get so excited. I wasn't volunteering for the position."

With his index finger pointing at her like the barrel of a shotgun, Kramer paced around the kitchen table again, his journey made in shuffling impatient steps. He circled the table twice before he spoke.

"You cleaned my home, washed my clothes and now you're cooking my dinner." Each word came at her like an accusation.

"Yes?"

"You can't possibly look at me with those big baby-blues of yours and expect me to believe that."

"Believe what?"

"That you're not applying for the job. From the moment we met, you've been doing all these... these sweet *girlie* things to entice me."

"Sweet girlie things?" Maryanne repeated, struggling to contain her amusement. "I don't think I understand."

"I don't expect you to admit it."

"I haven't the foggiest idea what you're talking about."

"You know," he accused once more with an angry shrug.

"Obviously I don't. What could I possibly have done to make you think that?"

"Sweet girlie things," he said again, but without the same conviction. He chewed on his bottom lip for a moment while he mulled the matter over. "All right, I'll give you an example—that perfume you're always wearing."

"Windchime? It's a light fragrance."

"I don't know the name of it. But it hangs around for an hour or so after you've left the room. You know that, and yet you wear it every time we're together."

"I've worn Windchime for years."

"That's not all," he continued quickly. "It's the way I catch you looking at me sometimes."

"Looking at you?" She folded her arms around her waist and rolled her eyes toward the ceiling.

"Yes," he returned, sounding even more peevish. He pressed his hand to his hip, cocked his chin at a regal angle and softly fluttered his thick eyelashes like fans.

Despite her efforts to hold in her amusement, Maryanne laughed outright. "I sincerely hope you're joking."

Kramer dropped his hand from his hip. "I'm not. You get this innocent look and your lips pout just so... Why, a man—any man—couldn't keep from wanting to kiss you."

"That's preposterous." But Maryanne instinctively pinched her lips together and closed her eyes.

Kramer's arm shot out. "That's another thing."

"What now?"

"The way you get this helpless flustered look and it's all a simpleminded male can do not to rush in and offer to take care of whatever's bothering you."

"By this time you should know I'm perfectly capable of taking care of myself," Maryanne felt obliged to remind him.

"You're a lamb among wolves," Kramer returned swiftly. "I don't know how long you intend to play out this silly charade, but personally I think you've overdone it now. This isn't your world, and the sooner you go back where you belong, the better it'll be."

"Better for whom?"

"Me!" he cried vehemently. "And for you," he added with less fervor, as though it was an afterthought. He coughed a couple of times and reached for a package of cough drops in the pocket of his plaid robe. Shaking one out, he popped it in his mouth with barely a pause.

"I don't think it's doing you any good to get so excited," Maryanne said with unruffled patience. "I was merely making an observation and it still stands. I believe you need a wife."

"Go observe someone else's life," he suggested, sucking madly on the cough drop.

"Aha!" she cried, waving her index finger at him. "How does it feel to have someone interfering in *your* life?"

Kramer frowned and Maryanne turned back to the stove. She lifted the lid from the soup to stir it briskly. Then she lowered the burner to simmer. When she was through, she saw with a glimmer of fun that Kramer was standing as far away from her as humanly possible, while still remaining in the same room.

"That's something else!" he cried. "You give the impression that you're in total agreement with whatever I'm saying and then go about doing exactly as you damn well please. I swear I've never met a more frustrating woman in my entire life."

"That's not true," Maryanne argued. "I quit my job at Rent-A-Maid because you insisted." It had worked out for the best, since she had more time for her writing now, but this wasn't the moment to mention it.

"Oh, right, bring that up. It's the only thing you've ever done that I wanted. I practically had to get down on my knees and beg you to leave that crazy job before you injured yourself."

"You didn't!"

"Trust me, it was a humbling experience and not one I intend to repeat. I've known you how long? A month? Lord, lord—" he paused to gaze at the ceiling "—it seems like an eternity."

"You're trying to make me feel guilty. It isn't going to work."

"Why should you feel anything of the sort? Just because living next to you is enough to drive a man to drink."

"You're the one who found me this place. If you don't like living next door to me, then I'm not the one to blame!"

"Don't remind me," he muttered.

The comment about Kramer finding himself a wife had been made in jest, a joke, but he'd certainly taken it seriously. In fact, he seemed to have strong feelings about the entire issue. Realizing her welcome had worn extremely thin, Maryanne headed for his apartment door. "Everything's under control here."

"Does that mean you're leaving?"

She hated the enthusiastic lift in his voice, as if he couldn't wait to be rid of her. Although he wasn't admitting it, she'd done him a good turn. Fair exchange, she supposed; Kramer had been generous enough to her over the past month.

"Yes, I'm leaving."

"Good." He didn't bother to disguise his delight.

"But I still think you'd do well to consider what I said." Maryanne had the irresistible urge to heap coals on the fires of his indignation. "A wife could be a great help to you."

Kramer frowned heavily, drawing his eyebrows into a deep V. "I think the modern woman would find your suggestion downright insulting."

"What? That you marry?"

"Exactly. Haven't you heard? A woman's place isn't in the home any longer. It's out there in the world, forging a career for herself. Living a fuller life, and all that. It's not doing the mundane tasks you're talking about."

"I wasn't suggesting you marry for the convenience of gaining a live-in housekeeper."

His brown eyes narrowed. "Then exactly what were you saying?"

"That you're a capable talented man," she explained. She glanced surreptitiously at his manuscript, still tidily stacked by the typewriter. "But unfortunately, that doesn't mean a whole lot if you don't have someone close—a friend, a companion, a . . . wife—to share it with."

"Don't you worry about me, Little Miss Muffet. I've lived my own life from the time I was thirteen. You may think I need someone, but let me assure you, I don't."

"You're probably right," she admitted reluctantly. She opened his door, then hesitated. "You'll call if you want anything?"

"No."

She released a short sigh of frustration. "That's what I thought. The soup should be done in about thirty minutes."

He nodded, then looking a bit chagrined, added, "I suppose I should thank you."

"I suppose you should, too, but it isn't necessary."

"What about the money you spent on groceries? You can't afford acts of charity, you know. Wait a minute and I'll—"

"Forget it," she snapped. "I can spend my money on whatever I damn well please. I'm my own person, remember? You can just owe me. Buy me dinner sometime." She left before he could say anything else.

Maryanne's own apartment felt bleak and lonely after Kramer's. The first thing she did was walk around turning on all the lights. No sooner had she finished when there was a loud knock at her door. She opened it to find Kramer standing there in his disreputable moth-eaten robe, glaring ferociously.

"Yes?" she inquired sweetly.

"You read my manuscript," he boomed in a voice that echoed like thunder off the apartment walls.

"I most certainly did not," she denied vehemently. She straightened her back as if to suggest she found the very question insulting.

Without waiting for an invitation, Kramer stalked into her living room, then whirled around to face her. "Admit it!"

Making each word as clear and distinct as possible, Maryanne said, "I did not read your precious manuscript. How could I possibly have cleaned up, done the laundry, prepared a big kettle of homemade soup, and still had time to read 212 pages of manuscript?''

"How did you know it was 212 pages?'' Sparks of reproach shot from his eyes.

"Ah—'' she swallowed uncomfortably ''—it was a guess, and from the looks of it, a good one.''

"It wasn't any guess.''

He marched toward her and for every step he took, she retreated two. "All right,'' she admitted guiltily, "I did look at it, but I swear I didn't read more than a few lines. I was straightening up the living room and...it was there, so I turned over the last page and read a couple of paragraphs.''

"Aha! Finally, the truth!'' Kramer pointed directly at her "You did read it!''

"Just a few lines,'' she repeated in a tiny voice, feeling completely wretched.

"And?'' His eyes softened.

"And what?''

"What did you think?'' He looked toward her expectantly, then frowned. "Never mind, I shouldn't have asked.''

Rubbing her palms together, Maryanne took one step forward. "Kramer, it was wonderful. Witty and terribly suspenseful and... I would have given anything to read more. But I knew I didn't dare because, well, because I was invading your privacy...which I didn't want to do, but I did and I really didn't want...that.''

"It is good, isn't it?'' he asked almost smugly, then his expression sobered as quickly as it had before.

She grinned, nodding enthusiastically. "Tell me about it.''

He seemed undecided, then launched excitedly into his idea. "It's about a Seattle newspaperman, Leo, who stumbles on a murder case. Actually, I'm developing a series with him as the main character. This one's not quite finished yet—as I'm sure you know."

"Is there a woman in Leo's life?"

"You're kidding, aren't you?"

Maryanne wasn't. The few lines she'd read had mentioned a Maddie who was apparently in danger. Leo had been frantic to save her.

"You had no business going anywhere near that manuscript," Kramer reminded her.

"I know, but the temptation was so strong. I shouldn't have peeked, I realize that, but I couldn't help myself. Kramer, I'm not lying when I say how good those few lines were. Do you have a publisher in mind? Because if you don't, I have several New York editor friends I could recommend and I know—"

"I'm not using you or any influence you may have in New York. I don't want anything to do with your father's publishing company. Understand?"

"Of course, but you're overreacting." He seemed to be doing a lot of that lately. "My father wouldn't stay in business long if he ordered the editors to purchase my friends' manuscripts, would he? Believe me, it would all be on the up and up, and if you've an idea for a series using Leo—"

"I said no."

"But—"

"I mean it, Annie. This is my book and I'll submit it myself without any help from you."

"If that's what you want," she concurred meekly.

"That's the way it's going to be." The stern unyielding look slipped back into place. "Now if you don't mind, I'll quietly go back to my messy little world, sans wife and countless interruptions from a certain neighbor.''

"I'll try not to bother you again," Maryanne said sarcastically, since he was the one who'd invaded *her* home this time.

"It would be appreciated," he said, apparently ignoring her tone.

"Your apartment is yours and mine is mine, and I'll uphold your privacy with the utmost respect," she continued, her voice still faintly mocking. She buried her hands in her pants pockets and her fingers closed around something cold and metallic.

"Good." Kramer was nodding. "Privacy, that's what we need."

"Um, Kramer..." She paused. "This is somewhat embarrassing, but it seems I have..." She hesitated a second time then resolutely squared her shoulders. "I suppose you'd appreciate it if I returned your keys, right?"

"My keys?" Kramer exploded.

"I just found them. They were in my pocket. You see, all you had in your refrigerator was one limp strand of celery and I couldn't very well make soup out of that so I had to go to the store and I didn't dare leave your door unlocked and—"

"You have my keys?"

"Yes."

He held out his palm, casting his eyes toward the ceiling. Feeling like a pickpocket caught in the act, Maryanne dropped the keys into his hand and stepped quickly back, almost afraid he was going to grab her shoulders and shake her. Which, of course, was ludicrous.

Kramer left immediately and Maryanne followed him to the door, staring out into the hallway as he walked back to his own apartment.

THE FOLLOWING THURSDAY, Maryanne was hurrying to get ready for work when the telephone rang. She frowned and stared at it, wondering if she dared take the time to answer. It might be Kramer, but every instinct she possessed told her otherwise. They hadn't spoken all week. Every afternoon, like clockwork, he'd arrived at Mom's Diner. More often than not, he ordered chili. Maryanne waited on him most of the time, but she might have been a robot for all the attention he paid her. His complete lack of interest dented her pride; still, his attitude shouldn't have come as any surprise.

"Hello," she said hesitantly, picking up the receiver.

"Maryanne," her mother responded, her voice rising with pleasure. "I can't believe I finally got hold of you. I've been trying for the past three days."

Maryanne immediately felt swamped by guilt. "You didn't leave a massage on my machine?"

"You know how I hate those things."

Maryanne did know that. She also knew she should have phoned her parents herself, but she wasn't sure how long she could continue with this farce. "Is everything all right?"

"Yes, of course. Your father's working too hard, but that's nothing new. The boys are busy with soccer and growing like weeds." Her mother's voice dipped slightly. "How's the job?"

"The job?"

"Your special assignment."

"Oh, that." Maryanne had rarely been able to fool her mother, and she could only wonder how well she was succeeding now. "It's going... well. I'm learning so much."

"I think you'll make a terrific investigative reporter, sweetie, and the secrecy behind this assignment makes it all the more intriguing. When are your father and I going to learn exactly what you've been doing? How I wish we'd never promised not to check up on your progress at the paper. We're both so curious."

"I'll be finished with it soon." Maryanne glanced at her watch and was about to close the conversation when her mother asked, "How's Kramer?"

"Kramer?" Maryanne's heart zoomed straight into her throat. She hadn't remembered mentioning him, and just hearing his name sent a feverish heat through her body.

"You seemed quite enthralled with him the last time we spoke, remember?"

"I was?"

"Yes, sweetie, you were. You claimed he was very talented, and although you were tight-lipped about it, I got the impression you were strongly attracted to this young man."

"Kramer's a good friend. But we argue more than anything."

Her mother chuckled. "Good."

"How could that possibly be good?"

"It means you're comfortable enough with each other to be yourselves, and that's a positive sign. Why, your father and I bickered like old fishwives when we first met. I swear there wasn't a single issue we could agree on." She sighed softly. "Then one day we looked at each other, and I knew then and there I was going to love this man for the rest of my life. And I have."

"Mom, it isn't like that with Kramer and me. I . . . I don't even think he likes me."

"Kramer doesn't like you?" her mother repeated. "Why, sweetie, that would be impossible."

Maryanne started to laugh then, because her mother was so obviously biased, yet sounded completely objective and matter-of-fact. It felt good to laugh again, good to find something amusing. She hadn't realized how melancholy she'd become since her last encounter with Kramer. He was still making such an effort to keep her at arm's length for fear . . . She didn't know exactly *what* he feared. Perhaps he was falling in love with her, but she'd noticed precious little evidence pointing to that conclusion. If anything, Kramer considered her an irritant in his life.

Maryanne spoke to her mother for a few more minutes, then rushed out the door, hoping she wouldn't be late for her shift at Mom's Place. Some investigative reporter she was!

At the diner, she slipped the apron around her waist and hurried out to help with the luncheon crowd. Waiting tables, she was learning quite a lot about character types. This could be helpful for a writer, she figured. Some of her customers were downright eccentric. She observed them carefully, wondering if Kramer did the same thing. But she wasn't going to think about Kramer. . . .

Halfway through her shift, she began to feel lightheaded and sick to her stomach.

"Are you feeling all right?" Barbara asked as she slipped past, carrying an order.

"I—I don't know."

"When was the last time you ate?"

"This morning. No," she corrected, "last night. I didn't have much of an appetite this morning."

"That's what I thought." Barbara set the hamburger and fries on the counter in front of her customer and walked back to Maryanne. "Now that I've got a good look at you, you do seem a bit peaked."

"I'm all right."

Hands on her hips, Barbara continued to study Maryanne as if memorizing every feature. "Are you sure?"

"I'm fine." She had the beginnings of a headache, but nothing she could really complain about. It probably hadn't been a good idea to skip breakfast and lunch, but she'd make up for it when she took her dinner break.

"I'm not sure I believe you," Barbara muttered, dragging out a well-used phone book. She flipped through the pages until she apparently found the number she wanted, then reached for the phone.

"Who are you calling?"

She held the receiver against her shoulder. "Kramer Adams, who else? Seems to me it's his turn to play nursemaid."

"Barbara, no!" She might not be feeling a hundred percent, but she wasn't all that sick, either. And the last person she wanted running to her rescue was Kramer. He'd only use it against her, as proof that she should go back to the cozy comfortable world of her parents. She'd almost proved she could live entirely on her own, without relying on interest from her trust fund.

"Kramer's not at the office," Barbara said a moment later, replacing the receiver. "I'll talk to him when he comes in later."

"No, you won't! Barbara, I swear to you I'll person-ally give your phone number to every trucker who comes into this place if you so much as say a single word to Kramer."

"Honey," the other waitress said, raising her eye-brows, "you'd be doing me a favor!"

Grumbling, Maryanne returned to her customers.

By closing time, however, she was feeling slightly worse. Not exactly sick, but not exactly herself, either. Barbara was watching Maryanne closely, regularly feeling her cheeks and forehead and muttering about her temperature. If there was one thing to be grateful for, it was the fact that Kramer hadn't shown up. Bar-bara insisted Maryanne leave a few minutes early and shooed her out the door. Had she been feeling better, Maryanne would have argued.

By the time she arrived back at her apartment, she knew beyond a doubt she was coming down with some kind of virus. Part of her would have liked to blame Kramer, but she was the one who'd let herself into his apartment. She was the one who'd lingered there, straightening up the place and staying far longer than necessary.

After a long hot shower, she put on her flannel pa-jamas and unfolded her bed, climbing quickly beneath the covers. She'd turned the television on for company and prepared herself a mug of soup. As she took her first sip, she heard someone knock at her door.

"Who is it?" she called out.

"Kramer."

"I'm in bed," she shouted.

"You've seen me in my robe. It's only fair I see you in yours," he yelled back.

Maryanne tossed aside her covers and sat up. "Go away."

A sharp pounding noise came from the floor, followed by an equally loud roar that proclaimed it time for "Jeopardy." Apparently, Maryanne's shouting match with Kramer was disrupting Mrs. McBride's favorite television show.

"Sorry." Maryanne cupped her hands over her mouth and yelled at the hardwood floor.

"Are you going to let me in, or do I have to get the passkey?" Kramer demanded.

Groaning, Maryanne shuffled across the floor in her giant fuzzy slippers and turned the lock. "Yes?" she asked with exaggerated patience.

For the longest moment, Kramer said nothing. He shoved his hands deep into the pockets of his beige raincoat. "How are you?"

Maryanne glared at him with all the indignation she could muster, which at the moment was considerable. "Do you mean to say you practically pounded down my door to ask me that?"

He didn't bother to answer, but walked into her apartment as though he had every right to do so. "Barbara phoned me."

"Oh, brother! And what exactly did she say?" She continued to hold open the door, hoping he'd get the hint and leave.

"That you caught my bug." His voice was rough with ill-disguised worry.

"Wrong. I felt a bit under the weather earlier, but I'm fine now." The last thing she wanted Kramer motivated by was guilt. He'd succeeded in keeping his distance up to now; if he decided to see her, she wanted to be sure his visit wasn't prompted by an overactive sense of responsibility.

"You look . . ."

"Yes?" she prompted.

His gaze skimmed her, from slightly damp hair to large fuzzy feet. "Fine," he answered softly.

"As you can see I'm really not sick, so you needn't concern yourself."

Her words were followed by a lengthy silence. Kramer turned as though to leave. Maryanne should have felt relieved to see him go, but instead she experienced the strangest sensation of loss. She longed to reach out a hand, ask him to stay, but she didn't have the courage.

She brushed the hair from her face and smiled, even though it was difficult to put on a carefree facade.

"I'll stop by in the morning and see how you're doing," Kramer said, hovering by the threshold.

"That won't be necessary."

He frowned. "When did you get so prickly?"

"When did you get so caring?" The words nearly caught in her throat and escaped on a whisper.

"I *do* care about you," he countered.

"Oh sure, the same way you'd care about an annoying younger sister. Believe me, Kramer, your message came through loud and clear. I'm not your type. Fine, I can accept that, because you're not my type, either." She didn't really think she had a type, but it sounded philosophical and went a long way toward salving her badly bruised ego. Kramer couldn't have made his views toward her any plainer had he rented a billboard. He'd even said he'd taken one look at her and immediately thought, "Here comes trouble."

She'd never been more attracted to a man in her life, and here she was, standing in front of him lying through her teeth, willing to walk across hot coals before she'd admit how she truly felt.

"So I'm not your type, either?" he asked, almost in a whisper.

Maryanne's heartbeat quickened. He studied her as intently as she studied him. He gazed at her mouth, then slipped his hand behind her neck and slowly, so very slowly, lowered his lips to hers.

He paused, their mouths a scant inch apart. He seemed to be waiting for her to pull away, withdraw from him. Everything inside her told her to do exactly that. He was only trying to humiliate her, wasn't he? Trying to prove how powerful her attraction to him was, how easily he could bend her will to his own.

And she was letting him.

Her heart was beating so furiously her body seemed to rock with the sheer force of it. Every throb seemed to drive her directly into his arms, right where she longed to be. She placed her palms against his chest and sighed as his mouth met hers. The touch of his lips felt warm and soft. And right.

His hand cradled her neck while his lips continued to move over hers in the gentlest explorations, as though he feared she was too delicate to kiss the way he wanted.

Gradually his hands slipped to her shoulders. He drew a ragged breath, then put his head back as he stared up at the ceiling. He exhaled slowly, deliberately.

It took all the restraint Maryanne possessed not to ask him why he was stopping. She wanted these incredible sensations to continue. She longed to explore the feelings his kiss produced and the complex responses she experienced deep within her body. Her pulse hammered erratically as she tried to control her breathing.

"Okay, now we've got that settled, I'll leave." He backed away from her.

"Got what settled?" she asked swiftly, then realized she was only making a bigger fool of herself. Naturally he was talking about the reason for this impromptu visit, which had been her health. Hadn't it? "Oh, I see."

"I don't think you do," Kramer said enigmatically. He turned and walked away.

CHAPTER EIGHT

"WHOSE TURN NEXT?" Maryanne asked. She and her two friends were sitting in the middle of her living-room floor, having a "pity party."

"I will," Carol Riverside volunteered eagerly. She ceremonially plucked a tissue from the box that rested in the center of their small circle, next to the lit candle. Their second large bottle of cheap wine was nearly empty, and the three of them were feeling no pain.

"For years I've wanted to write a newspaper column of my own," Carol said, squaring her shoulders and hauling in a huge breath. "But it's not at all what I thought it'd be like. I ran out of ideas for things to write about after the first week."

"Ah," Maryanne sighed sympathetically.

"Ah," Barbara echoed.

"That's not all," Carol said sadly. "I never realized the world was so full of critics. No one seems to agree with me. I—I didn't know Seattle had so many cantankerous readers. I try, but it's impossible to make everyone happy. What happens is that some of the people like me some of the time and all the rest hate everything I write." She glanced up. "Except the two of you, of course."

Maryanne nodded her head so hard she nearly toppled over. She spread her hands out at either side in an effort to maintain her balance. The wine made her yawn, loudly.

Apparently in real distress, Carol dabbed at her eyes. "Being a columnist is hard work and nothing like I'd always dreamed." The edges of her mouth turned downward. "I don't even like writing anymore," she sobbed.

"Isn't that a pity!" Maryanne cried, ritually tossing her tissue into the center of the circle. Barbara followed suit, and then they both patted Carol gently on the back.

Carol brightened once she'd finished. "I don't know what I'd do without the two of you. You and Betty are my very best friends in the whole world," she announced.

"Barbara," Maryanne corrected. "Your very best friend's name is Barbara."

The three of them looked at each other and burst into gales of laughter. Maryanne hushed them by waving her hands. "Stop! We can't allow ourselves to become giddy. A pity party doesn't work if all we do is laugh. We've got to remember this is sad and serious business."

"Sad and serious," Barbara agreed, sobering. She reached for a fresh tissue and clenched it in her hand, waiting for the others to share their sorrows and give her a reason to cry.

"Whose idea was the wine?" Maryanne wanted to know, taking a quick sip.

Carol blushed. "I thought it would be less fattening than the chocolate ice-cream bars you planned to serve."

"Hey," Barbara said, narrowing her eyes at Mary-anne. "You haven't said anything about your problem."

Maryanne suddenly found it necessary to pick lint from her jeans. Sharing what disturbed her most was a little more complicated than being disappointed in her job or complaining about fingernails that cracked all too easily, as Barbara had done. She hadn't sold a single article since she quit the paper, or even received a positive response to one of her queries. But worst of all she was falling in love with Kramer. He felt something for her, too—she knew that—but he was fighting her every step of the way. Fighting her and fighting himself.

He was attracted to her, he couldn't deny it, although he'd tried to, more than once. When they were alone together, the tension seemed to throb between them.

He was battling the attraction so hard he'd gone as far as arranging a date for her with another man. Since the evening they'd met, Kramer had insulted her, ha-rangued her and lectured her. He'd made it plain that he didn't want her around. And yet there were times when he sought out her company. He argued with her at every opportunity, took it upon himself to be her guardian, and yet . . .

"Maryanne?" Carol said, studying her with concern. "What's wrong?"

"Kramer Adams," she whispered. Lifting her wine-glass, she took a small swallow, hoping that would give her the courage to continue.

"I should have guessed," Carol muttered, frowning. "From the moment you moved in here, next door to that madman, I just knew he'd cause you nothing but problems.''

Her friend's opinion of Kramer had never been high and Maryanne had to bite back the urge to defend him.

''Tell us everything,'' Barbara said, drawing up her knees and leaning back against the sofa.

''There isn't much to tell.''

''He's the one who got you into this craziness in the first place, remember?'' Carol pointed out righteously—as if Maryanne needed reminding. Carol then turned to Barbara and began to explain to the older woman how it had all started. ''Kramer wrote a derogatory piece about Maryanne in his column a while back, implying she was a spoiled debutante, and she took it to heart and decided to prove him wrong.''

''He didn't mean it. In fact, he's regretted every word of that article.'' This time Maryanne felt obliged to defend him. As far as she was concerned, this was old business, already resolved. It was the unfinished business, the things happening between them now, that bothered her most.

The denial. The refusal on both their parts to accept the feelings they shared. Only a few days earlier, Maryanne had tried to convince Kramer he wasn't her type and nothing about them was compatible. He'd been only too eager to agree.

But they'd been drawn together, virtually against their wills, by an attraction so overwhelming, so inevitable, they were powerless against it. This sensual and emotional awareness of one another seemed more intense every time they met. This feeling couldn't be anything except love.

''You're among friends, so tell us everything,'' Barbara pressed, handing Maryanne the entire box of tissues. "Remember, I've known Kramer for years, so nothing you say is going to shock me."

"For one thing, he's impossible," Maryanne whispered, having difficulty expressing her thoughts.

"He deserves to be hanged from the closest tree," Carol said scornfully.

"And at the same time he's wonderful," Maryanne concluded, ignoring Carol's comment.

"You're not..." Carol paused, her face tightening as if she was having trouble forming the words. "You don't mean to suggest you're falling in—" she swallowed "—*love* with him, are you?"

"I don't know." Maryanne clenched the soggy tissue in her hands. "But I think I might be."

"Oh, no," Carol cried, covering her mouth with both hands, "you've got to do something quick. A man like Kramer Adams eats little girls like you for breakfast. He's cynical and sarcastic and—"

"Talented and generous," Maryanne finished for her.

"You're not thinking clearly. It probably has something to do with that fever you had. You've got to remember the facts. Kramer insulted you in print, seriously insulted you, and then tried to make up for it. You're mistaking this small attack of conscience as something more, and that could be dangerous." Awkwardly, Carol rose to her feet and started pacing.

"He's probably one of the most talented writers I've ever read," Maryanne continued, undaunted by her friend's concerns. "Every time I read his work, I can't help being awed."

"All right," Carol said, "I'll concede he does possess a certain amount of creative talent, but that doesn't change who or what he is. Kramer Adams is a bad-tempered egotistical self-centered...grouch."

"I hate to say this," Barbara said softly, shaking her head, "but Carol's right. Kramer's been eating at Mom's Place for as long as I've worked there, and that's three years. I feel like I know him better than you do, and he's everything Carol says. But you know, underneath it all, there's more to him. Oh, he'd like everyone to believe he's this macho guy. He plays that role to the hilt, but after you've been around him awhile, anyone with a lick of sense would know it's all a game to him."

"I told you he's wonderful!" Maryanne exclaimed.

"The man's a constant," Carol insisted. "Constantly in a bad mood, constantly making trouble, constantly getting involved in matters that are none of his business. Maryanne here is the perfect example. He should never have written that column about her." Carol plopped back down and jerked half a dozen tissues from the box in quick succession. She handed them to Maryanne. "You've got blinders on where he's concerned. Take it from me, a woman can't allow herself to become emotionally involved with a man she plans to change."

"I don't want to change Kramer."

"You don't?" Carol echoed, her voice low and disbelieving. "You mean to say you like him as he is?"

"You just don't know him the way I do," Maryanne said. "Kramer's truly generous. Did either of you know he's become sort of a father figure for the teenagers in this neighborhood? He's their friend in the very best sense. He keeps tabs on them and makes sure no one gets involved in drugs or is lured into gang activities. The kids around here idolize him."

"Kramer Adams does that?" Carol sounded skeptical. She arched her brows as though she couldn't completely trust Maryanne's observations.

"When Barbara told him I was coming down with a virus, he came over to check on me and—"

"As well he should!" Barbara declared. "He was the one who gave you that germ in the first place."

"I'm not entirely sure I caught it from him."

Carol and Barbara exchanged a look. Slowly each shook her head, and then all three shared a warm smile.

"I think we might be too late," Barbara said theatrically to Carol, speaking from the side of her mouth.

"She's showing all the signs," Carol agreed solemnly.

"You're right, I fear," Barbara responded in kind. "She's already in love with him."

"Good grief, no," Carol wailed, pressing her hands to her mouth. "Say it isn't so. She's too young and vulnerable."

"It's a pity, such a pity."

"I can't help but agree. Maryanne is much too sweet for Kramer Adams. I just hope he appreciates her."

"He won't," Carol muttered, reverting to her normal voice, "but then no man ever fully appreciates a woman."

"What about Alan Alda?" Maryanne demanded.

"Maybe him."

"Oh, sure, Alan," Carol agreed.

"It's such a pity men act the way they do."

"Some men," Maryanne added.

Carol and Barbara dabbed their eyes and solemnly tossed the used tissues into the growing heap in the middle of their circle.

The plan had been to gather all the used tissues and ceremonially dump them in the toilet, flush their "pity pot," and then celebrate all the good things in their lives.

The idea for this little party had been an impromptu one of Maryanne's on a lonely Friday night. She'd been feeling blue and friendless and decided to look for a little innocent fun. She'd phoned Carol and learned she was a weekend widow; her husband had gone fishing with some cronies. Barbara had thought the idea was a good one herself, since she'd just broken her longest fingernail and was in the mood for a shoulder to cry on.

A pity party seemed just the thing to help three lonely women make it through a bleak Friday night.

MARYANNE AWOKE Saturday morning with a humdinger of a headache. Wine and the ice cream they'd had at the end of the evening definitely didn't mix.

If her head hadn't been throbbing so painfully, she might have recognized sooner that her apartment had no heat. Her cantankerous radiator was acting up again. It did that some mornings, but she'd always managed to coax it back to life with a few well-placed whacks. The past few days had been unusually cold for early November—well below freezing at night.

She reached for her robe and slippers, bundling herself up like a December baby out in her first snowstorm. Cupping her hands over her mouth, she blew until a frosty mist formed.

A quickly produced cup of coffee with two extrastrength aspirin took the edge off her headache. Maryanne shivered while she slipped into jeans, sweatshirt and a thick winter coat. She suspected she resembled someone who was preparing to join an Arctic expedition.

She fiddled with the radiator, twisting the knobs and slamming her hand against the side, but the only results were a couple of rattles and a hollow clanking sound.

Not knowing what else to try, she got out her heavy cast-iron skillet and banged it against the top of the rad in hopes of reviving the aging pipes.

The sound was deafening, vibrating through the room like a jet aircraft crashing through the sound barrier. If that wasn't enough, Maryanne's entire body began to quiver, starting at her arm and spreading outward in a rippling effect that caused her arms and legs to tremble.

"What the hell's going on over there?" Kramer shouted from the other side of the wall. He didn't wait for her to answer and a couple of seconds later came barreling through her front door, wild-eyed and disheveled.

"What... Where?" He was carrying a baseball bat, and stalked to the middle of her apartment, scanning the interior for what Maryanne could only assume were foreign invaders.

"I don't have any heat," she announced, tucking the thin scarf more tightly around her ears.

Kramer blinked. She'd apparently woken him from a sound sleep. He was barefooted and dressed in pajama bottoms, and although he wore a shirt, it was unbuttoned, revealing a broad muscular chest dusted with curly black hair.

"What's with you? Are you going to a costume party?"

"Believe me, this is no party. I'm simply trying to keep warm."

His gaze lowered to the heavy skillet in her hand. "Do you plan to cook on that radiator?"

"I might, but I can't seem to get it to work. In case you hadn't noticed there isn't any heat in this place."

Kramer set the baseball bat aside and moved to the far wall to look over the radiator. "What's wrong with it?"

How like a man to ask stupid questions! If Mary-anne had *known* what was wrong with it, she wouldn't be standing there shivering, with a scarf swaddling her face like an old-time remedy for toothache.

"How in heaven's name am I supposed to know?" she answered testily.

"What went on here last night, anyway? A wake?"

She glanced at the mound of tissues and shrugged. He was scanning the area as if it were a crime scene and he should take caution not to stumble over a dead body.

Walking across the living room, he picked up the two empty wine bottles and held them aloft for her inspection, pretending to be shocked.

"Very funny." She put the skillet down and removed the bottles from his hands, to be deposited promptly in the garbage.

"So you had a party and I wasn't invited." He made it sound as though he'd missed the social event of the year.

Maryanne sighed loudly. "If you must know, Carol, Barbara and I had a pity party."

"A what? You're kidding, right?" He didn't bother to hide his mocking grin.

"Never mind." She should have realized he'd only poke fun at her. "Can you figure out how to get this thing working before the next ice age?"

"Here, give me a shot at it." He gently patted the top of the radiator as he knelt in front of it. "Okay, ol' Betsy, we're trusting you to be good." He began fiddling with knobs, still murmuring ridiculous endearments—like a cowboy talking to his horse.

"It doesn't do any good to talk to an inanimate object," she advised primly, standing behind him.

"You want to do this?"

"No," she muttered. Having Kramer in her home, dressed in his night clothes, did something odd to her, sent her pulse skittering erratically. She deliberately allowed her attention to wander to the scene outside her window. The still-green lawns of Volunteer Park showed in the distance and she pretended to be absorbed in their beauty.

"I thought I told you to keep that door chain in place." He mentioned casually as he worked. "This isn't The Seattle."

"Do you honestly think you need to remind me of that now?" She rubbed her hands together, hoping to generate some warmth before her fingers went numb.

"There," he said, sounding satisfied. "All she needed was a little bit of loving care."

"Thanks," Maryanne said with relief.

"No problem, only the next time something like this happens don't try to fix it yourself."

"Translated, that means I shouldn't try to fix the radiator again while *you're* trying to sleep."

"Right."

She smiled up at him, her eyes alive with appreciation. He really had been good to her from the day she'd moved in—before then, too. Discounting what he'd written about her in his column, of course. And even that had ended up having a positive effect.

It had been a week since she'd last seen him. A long week. A lonely week. Until now, she'd hardly been able to admit, even to herself, how much she'd missed him. Standing there as he was, Maryanne was stuck by just how really attractive she found him. If only he'd taken time to button his shirt! She reveled in his lean strength and his aura of unquestionable authority—and that chest of his was driving her to distraction.

She wasn't the only one enthralled. Kramer was staring at her, too. The silence lingered between them, lengthening moment by moment as they gazed into each other's eyes.

"I have to go," he finally said, breaking eye contact by glancing past her, out the window.

"Right. I—I understand," she stammered, stepping back. Her hands swung at her sides as she followed him to the door. "I really do appreciate this." Already she could feel the warmth spilling into her apartment. And none too soon, either.

"Just remember to keep the door locked."

She grinned and mockingly saluted him. "Aye, aye, sir."

He left then. Maryanne hated to see him go, hated to see him walk away from her, and yet it seemed he was continually doing exactly that.

LATER THAT SAME AFTERNOON, after she'd finished her errands, Maryanne was strolling through the park when a soft feminine voice spoke from behind her.

Maryanne turned around and waved when she discovered Gloria, the teenager she'd met here earlier. But this time Gloria wasn't alone.

"This is my little sister, Katie, the pest," Gloria explained. "She's three."

"Hello, Katie," Maryanne said, smiling.

"Why am I a pest?" Katie asked, gazing at Gloria, but apparently not offended that her older sister referred to her that way.

"Because." Looking annoyed, the teenager shrugged in the same vague manner Maryanne had so often seen in her younger brothers. "Katie's three and every other word is 'why.' Why this? Why that? It's enough to drive a person straight to the loony bin."

"I have brothers, so I know exactly what you mean."

"You do?"

"They're several years younger than I am. Trust me, I know exactly what you're talking about."

"Did your brothers want to go every place you did? And did your mother make you take them even if it was a terrible inconvenience?"

Maryanne tried to disguise a smile. "Sometimes."

"Eddie wanted me to come and watch him play basketball this afternoon with Mr. Adams, and I had to drag Katie along because she wanted to come to the park, too. My mom pressured me into bringing her. I didn't even get a chance to say no." Gloria made it sound as if she were being forced to swim across Puget Sound with the three-year-old clinging to her back.

"I'm not a pest," Katie insisted now, flipping her braid over one shoulder in a show of defiance. Looking up at Maryanne, the little girl carefully manipulated her fingers and proudly exclaimed, "I'm three."

"Three?" Maryanne repeated, raising her eyebrows, feigning surprise. "Really? I would have thought you were four or five."

Katie grinned delightedly. "I'm nearly four, you know."

"Mr. Adams is already here," Gloria said, brightening. She frowned as she glanced down at her little sister and jerked the small arm in an effort to hurry her along. "Come on, Katie, we have to hurry. Eddie wanted me to watch him play ball."

"Why?"

Gloria groaned. "See what I mean?"

"You go on," Maryanne said, offering Katie her hand. The youngster obediently slipped her small hand into Maryanne's much larger one, willingly abandoning her cranky older sister. "Katie and I will follow behind."

Gloria looked surprised by the offer. "You mean you don't mind? I mean, Katie is my responsibility and it wouldn't be fair to palm her off on you. You're not going to kidnap her or anything, are you? I mean, I know you're not—you're Mr. Adams's friend. I wouldn't let her go with just anyone, you know. But if anything happened to her, my mother would have my neck."

"I promise to take the very best care of her."

Gloria grinned, looking sheepish for having suggested anything else. "You're sure you don't mind?"

"I don't mind in the least. I don't think Katie does, either. Is that right, Katie?"

"Why?"

"Are you really sure? Okay, then..." Once she'd offered a token protest Gloria raced off to join her friends.

Katie was content to skip and hop at Maryanne's side until they reached a huge pile of leaves under a chestnut tree. Almost before Maryanne realized it, Katie had slipped away from her. The child raced toward the leaves, bunching as many as she could in her small arms and carrying them back to Maryanne as though presenting her with the rarest of jewels.

"Look," she cried happily. "Leafs."

"Leaves," Maryanne corrected, bending over and grabbing an armful herself. She tossed them into the air and grinned as Katie leapt up to catch as many as she could and in the process dropped the armload she was holding.

Laughing Maryanne clasped the child by the waist and swung her around, while Katie shrieked with delight. Dizzy, Maryanne leaned against the tree in an effort to regain her equilibrium and her breath.

It was then she noticed that Kramer had stopped playing and was standing alone in the middle of the basketball court, staring at her. The game was going on all around him, youths scattering in one direction and then the other, racing from one end of the court and back again. Kramer seemed oblivious to them and to the game—to everything but her.

A tall boy bumped into him from behind and Kramer stumbled. Maryanne gasped, fearing he might fall, but he caught himself in time. Without a pause, he rejoined the game, racing down the court at breakneck speed. He stole the ball and made a slam dunk, coming down hard on the pavement.

Gloria ran back toward Maryanne and Katie. "I thought you said you and Mr. Adams were just friends?" she teased. She was grinning in a way that suggested she wasn't about to be fooled again. "He nearly got creamed because he couldn't take his eyes off you.''

With Katie on her lap, Maryanne sat beside the teenage girls watching the game. Together she and the three-year-old became Kramer's personal cheering squad, but whether or not he appreciated their efforts, she didn't know. He didn't give a single indication he heard them.

When the game was finished, Kramer walked breathlessly off the court. His gray sweatshirt was ringed with perspiration, and his face was red and damp from the sheer physical exhaustion of keeping up with kids half his age.

For an anxious moment, Maryanne assumed he was planning to ignore her and simply walk away. But after he'd stopped at the water fountain, he walked over to the bench where she and Katie were sitting.

He slumped down beside her, disheveled and still breathing hard. "What are you doing here?" he grumbled.

"I happened to be in the park," she answered, feeling self-conscious now and unsure. "You don't need to worry, Kramer. I didn't follow you."

"I didn't think you had."

"You look nice in blue," he said hoarsely, then cleared his throat as if he hadn't meant to say that, as if he wanted to withdraw the words.

"Thanks." The blue sweater was one of her favorites. She'd worn her long wool coat and was surprised he'd even noticed the periwinkle-blue sweater beneath.

"Hello, Katie."

Katie beamed, reaching out both arms for Kramer to lift her up, which he did. The little girl hugged him quickly, then leapt off the bench and ran to her sister, who stood talking to her boyfriend.

"You're good with children," Kramer said. His voice fell slightly, as though the fact surprised him.

"I do have a knack with them. I always have." She had been much-sought as a baby-sitter by her parents' friends and for a time had considered becoming a teacher. If she'd pursued that field of study she would have preferred to teach kindergarten. She found five-year-olds, with their eagerness to learn about the world, delightful. A couple of articles she'd written the week before were geared toward children's magazines. If only she'd hear something soon. It seemed to take so long.

"How many years of your life did you lose this time?" Maryanne asked teasingly.

"Another two or three, at least."

He smiled at her and it was that rare special smile he granted her only in those brief moments when his guard was lowered. His resistance to the attraction he felt to her was at its weakest point, and they both knew it.

Maryanne went still, almost afraid to move or speak for fear of ruining the moment. His eyes, so warm and gentle, continued to hold hers. When she tried to breath, the air seemed to catch in her lungs.

"Maryanne." Her name was little more than a whisper.

"Yes?"

He raked his hand through his hair, then looked away. "Nothing. Never mind."

"What is it?" she pressed, unwilling to let the matter drop.

The muscles along the side of his jaw clenched. "I said it was nothing," he answered gruffly.

Maryanne gazed down at her hands, feeling an overwhelming sense of frustration and despair. The tension between them was so thick she could taste it, but nothing she could say or do would alter that. If anything, her efforts would only make it worse.

"Hey, Kramer," Eddie called out, loping toward them. "What's with you, man?" He laughed, tossing his basketball from one hand to the other. "You nearly lost that game because you couldn't take your eyes off your woman."

Kramer scowled at the youth. "You looking for a rematch?"

"Any time you want."

"Not today." Shaking his head, Kramer slowly pushed the sleeves of his sweatshirt past his elbows.

"Right," Eddie said with a knowing laugh. "I didn't think so, with your woman here and all."

"Maryanne isn't my woman," Kramer informed him curtly, his frown darkening.

"Right," Eddie responded. "Hey, dude, this is me, Eddie. Can't fool me! You practically went comatose when you saw her. I don't blame you, though. She ain't bad. So when are you two getting married?"

CHAPTER NINE

"I'VE CHANGED MY MIND," Barbara announced at closing time Monday evening.

Maryanne was busy refilling the salt and pepper shakers and reloading the napkin holders. "About what?" she asked absently, stuffing napkins into the small chrome canisters with practiced ease.

"You and Kramer."

If Barbara hadn't had Maryanne's attention earlier, she did now. Kramer had left the restaurant about forty minutes earlier, after having his customary meal of chili and coffee. He'd barely said two words to Maryanne the whole time he was there. He'd buried his face in the evening edition of the *Sun* and done a brilliant job of pretending he didn't know her.

"What about us?" Maryanne's expression might have remained aloof, but her heart was pounding furiously.

"Since the night of our pity party, I've had a change of heart. You're exactly the right kind of woman for Kramer. The two of you . . . balance each other. At first I agreed with Carol. My opinion of Kramer isn't as negative as hers, but you have to remember that those two work for rival papers. At any rate, I was concerned. You *are* really sweet."

Maryanne winced at the "sweet." It rather sounded as though friendship with her was like falling into a jar of honey.

"And now?"

"I don't know exactly what changed my mind. Partly it was watching Kramer when he was here. I got quite a kick out of him."

"How do you mean?"

Barbara's grin was broad as she continued to wipe the counter, her movements slow as if her thoughts were distracting her. "I swear that man couldn't keep his eyes off you."

Maryanne was puzzled. "What are you talking about? Kramer didn't look my way once."

"Oh, he'd scowl every time you were close, but behind that cross look of his was an intensity I can't ever remember seeing in him. It was like he had to come in and get his daily fix of you."

Maryanne's heart couldn't decide whether to lift with happiness or sink with doubt. "You're wrong. Other than ordering his meal, he didn't even speak to me. I might as well have been a robot."

"That's what he'd like you to believe."

"He was reading the paper," Maryanne countered. "The same way he reads it every time he comes here."

"Correction," Barbara said, and her face broke into a spontaneous smile. "He *pretended* to be reading the paper, but when you weren't looking, his eyes were following you like a hawk."

"Oh, Barbara, did he really?" It seemed almost more than she dared hope for. He'd hardly spoken to her in the past few days, and he seemed to be avoiding her. The kids in the park had taken to teasing them about being sweethearts and asking pointed questions, and

Kramer had practically fallen all over himself denying that they were anything more than friends.

"It's more than just the way he was watching you," Barbara said thoughtfully, slipping onto a stool. "Have you read his columns the past couple of weeks?"

Naturally Maryanne had, more impressed by his work every time she did. The range of his talent and the power of his writing were unmistakable. Within a few years, if not sooner, she expected his newspaper column to be picked up for syndication.

"Lately, I've noticed something unusual about his writing," Barbara continued, still clutching the dishrag. "That cynical edge of his—it isn't quite as sharp. His writing's less sarcastic now. I heard one of my customers comment earlier today that Kramer's going soft on us. I hadn't thought about it much until then, but Ernie's right. I don't know what's made the difference, but I figure it must be love. Oh, I doubt there's much in this life that's going to change Kramer Adams. He'll always be stubborn as a mule, headstrong and temperamental. That's just part of his nature. But mark my words, he's in love."

"But what you said earlier, about us being so different..."

"You are, with you so nice and all, and Kramer such a grouch. At least he likes to pretend he's one. You and I both know better, but most folks don't."

"And?" Maryanne probed.

"And, well, it seemed to me the two of you fit together perfectly. Like two pieces of a puzzle."

It seemed that way to Maryanne, too.

"You heard, didn't you?" Barbara muttered, abruptly changing the subject.

Maryanne nodded. Mom's Place was going to close the following month for remodeling.

"What are you going to do?"

Maryanne didn't know yet. "Find a temporary job, I suppose. What about you?" By then, she should have sold a few of the articles she'd submitted. At least she hadn't been rejected yet. She should be hearing any time.

"I'm not all that concerned about taking a month or so off work," Barbara returned, her look thoughtful. "I could use a vacation, especially over the holidays. I was thinking of staying home and baking Christmas gifts this year. My fudge is out of this world."

"I suppose I should start looking for another job now." Maryanne was already worried about meeting expenses. Mom's Place couldn't have chosen a worse time to close.

A HALF HOUR LATER, she was waiting for the bus, her mind spinning with what Barbara had said. The diner's closing was a concern, but Barbara's comments about Kramer gladdened Maryanne's heart.

Kramer did feel something for her, something more powerful than he dared let on.

She supposed she should confront him with it, force him to acknowledge his feelings. A brief smile crossed her lips as she envisioned what would happen if she actually did such a thing. She nearly laughed out loud at the thought.

Kramer would deny it, of course, loudly and vehemently, and she'd have to counteract with a loud argument of her own. The smile appeared again. Her decision was made.

Feeling almost light-headed, Maryanne glanced down the street, eager for the bus to arrive so she could get home. The first thing she intended to do was march into Kramer's apartment and demand the truth. If he tried to ignore her, as he usually did, then she had the perfect solution.

She'd kiss him.

A kiss would silence his protests in the most effective way she could imagine. Maryanne felt herself almost melt at the thought. Being kissed by Kramer, being held in his arms, was like walking through the gates of an undiscovered paradise. Just remembering those moments made her feel faint with desire, weak with excitement. When they broke apart she was always left restless and impatient for something she couldn't quite identify. He seemed to experience the same regrets, Maryanne remembered hopefully.

Cheered by the thought, she nearly applauded when her bus arrived. The ride passed quickly and she hurried into the building, eager to see Kramer.

Consumed by her sense of purpose, she went directly to his apartment. She stood in front of his door, took several deep breaths, then knocked politely. No answer. She tried again, harder this time.

"Who is it?" Kramer growled from the other side.

"Maryanne. I want to talk to you."

"I'm busy."

She was only a little discouraged by his unfriendliness. "This'll just take a minute."

The door was yanked opened with excessive force. Kramer stood before her, dressed in a black tuxedo and white cummerbund, looking so devilishly handsome that he caught her completely by surprise. Her mouth sagged open.

"Yes?" he asked crossly.

"Hello, Kramer," she said, aware that her mission had been thwarted. Nothing he could have said or done would have affected her as profoundly as finding him dressed like this. Because it meant he was going out on a date.

"Hello," he said, tugging at the cuffs of his jacket, adjusting the fit. He frowned, apparently waiting for her to say something.

"Uh..." She tried to gather her scattered composure, and finally managed to squeak, "You're going out?"

He scowled. "I don't dress like this for a jaunt to the movies."

"No, I don't suppose you do."

"You wanted something?"

She'd been so confident, so sure she was doing the right thing. But now, seeing Kramer looking more dressed up and formal than he'd ever looked for her, she found herself speechless.

She couldn't help wondering where he was going—and with whom. The "with whom" part bothered her the most.

He glanced pointedly at his wristwatch. "How long is this going to take?" he asked coolly. "I'm supposed to pick up Prudence in fifteen minutes."

"Prudence?" His face, tight with impatience, drew her full attention. *Prudence,* her mind repeated. He'd tossed the name at her like a hand grenade. Who was this woman?

Then in a flash, Maryanne knew. It was all she could do not to laugh and inform him that his little plan just wasn't working. No imaginary date was going to make *her* jealous.

He wasn't seeing anyone named Prudence. Good grief, if he had to invent a name, the least he could have done was come up with something a little more plausible than Prudence.

In fact, now that she thought about it, Maryanne remembered Kramer casually mentioning a week or so earlier that he'd been asked to speak at a Chamber of Commerce banquet. There had also been a notice in the paper. Who did he think he was kidding!

Of course he intended her to believe he was dating another woman. That was supposed to discourage her, she guessed. Except that it didn't.

"It wasn't important..." she said, gesturing vaguely. "The radiators were giving me a little trouble this morning, but I'll manage. I was planning to go out tonight myself."

His eyes connected with hers. "Another pity party?"

"Not this time." She considered announcing she had a hot date herself, but that would have been carrying this farce a little too far. "Barbara and I will probably go to a movie."

"Sounds like fun."

"I'm sure it will be." She smiled up at him, past the square cut of his jaw to his incredibly dark eyes. "Have a good time with... Prudence," she said with a bright knowing smile.

Holding back a laugh, she returned to her own apartment. The rat. The low-down dirty rat! He was pretending to escort some imaginary woman to a fancy affair. Oh, he'd like nothing better than for Maryanne to think he considered her a pest. But she knew that wasn't quite the case.

Where was the man who'd rushed to her rescue when the pipes needed a little coaxing? Where was the man who'd nearly been run over on a basketball court when he saw her standing on the sidelines? Where was the man who'd tried to set her up with someone else he thought more suitable? Kramer Adams had just proved what she'd suspected all along. He was a coward—at least when it came to love.

Depressed, Maryanne slowly crossed the living room and sank onto her sofa, trying to gather her wits. Ten minutes later, she still sat there, mulling things over and feeling sorry for herself, when she heard Kramer's door open and close. She immediately perked up, wondering if he'd had a change of heart. He seemed to pause for a moment outside her door, but any second thoughts he must be having didn't last long.

Barbara phoned soon after, full of apologies, to cancel their movie plans, so Maryanne spent the evening drowning her sorrows in television reruns and slices of cold pizza.

She must have fallen asleep because a harsh ringing jolted her awake a couple of hours later. She leapt off the sofa and stumbled dazedly around before she realized the sound came from the phone. She rushed across the room.

A greeting had barely left her lips when her father's booming voice assailed her.

"Where the hell are you?"

"Hello, Dad," Maryanne managed, her heart sinking. How like him to get to the subject at hand without anything in the way of preliminaries. "How are you, too?"

"I want to know where you're living and I want to know right now!"

"I beg your pardon?" she asked, stalling for time. Obviously her father had discovered her small deception.

"I talked to the managing editor of the *Seattle Review* this morning and he told me you haven't worked there in weeks. He said you'd quit. Now, I want to know what this craziness is you've been feeding your mother and me about a special assignment."

"Uh..." By now, Maryanne was awake enough to know her father wasn't in any mood to listen to excuses.

"You lied to us, girl."

"Not exactly..." She paused, searching for the right words. "It was more a case of omission, don't you think?"

"You've had us worried sick. We've been trying to get hold of you all afternoon. Where were you? And who the hell is Kramer Adams?"

"Kramer Adams?" she echoed, playing dumb, which at first point wasn't all that difficult.

"Your mother mentioned his name, and when I spoke to the paper, some woman named...Riverside, Carol Riverside, claimed this was his fault."

"Dad, listen, it's all rather complicated, so I think—"

"I don't want excuses, I want facts. You decided to work on the other side of the country. Against my better judgment, I arranged it for you with the promise I wouldn't intrude—and look where it's got me! To have you deceive us by—"

"Dad, please, just settle down."

He seemed to be making an effort to calm himself, but more than likely the effort was thanks to her mother. Maryanne could hear her arguing softly in the background.

"Can I explain?" she asked, waiting a moment or two for the tension to ease, although she wasn't sure what to say, what excuses she could possible offer.

"You can try to explain, but I doubt it'll do any good," he answered gruffly.

Now that she had the floor, Maryanne floundered.

"I take it this all revolves around that columnist friend of yours from the *Sun*?" her father asked. "That Kramer character?"

"Well, yes," Maryanne admitted reluctantly. But she didn't feel she could place the entire blame on him. "Leaving the paper was my decision—"

"Where are you living?"

That was one of several questions Maryanne was hoping to avoid. "I—I rented an apartment."

"You were in an apartment before. It doesn't make the least bit of sense for you to move. The Seattle has a reputation for excellence."

"Yes, Dad, I know, but moving was necessary." She didn't go on to explain why. She didn't want to mislead her father more than she had already. But at the same time, if she told him she couldn't afford to continue living at The Seattle, he'd certainly demand an explanation.

"That doesn't explain a damn thing," Samuel Simpson boomed.

Maryanne held the phone away from her ear and sighed heavily. This conversation couldn't have come at a worse time. She was groggy from her nap and discouraged by her relationship with Kramer. To complicate matters, she was truly in love for the first time in her life. Loving someone shouldn't be this difficult!

"I insist you tell me what's going on," her father said, in the tone of voice she remembered from childhood confrontations about missed curfews and other transgressions.

She tried again. "It's not that easy to explain."

"You have three seconds, young lady, to tell me why you've lied to your parents."

"I apologize for that. I've felt horrible about it, I really have, but I didn't want to say anything for fear you'd worry."

"Of course we'd worry! Now tell me exactly what it is we should be worrying about."

"Dad, honestly, I'm over twenty-one. I should be able to live and work where I please. You can't keep me your little girl forever." This conversation was not only reminiscent of several she'd had with Kramer, it was one she should have had with her father years ago.

"I demand to know why you quit the paper!"

Maryanne refused to be intimidated. "I already explained that. I had another job."

"Obviously you're doing something you're too ashamed to tell your parents."

"I'm not ashamed! It's nothing illegal. Besides, I happen to like what I do, and I've managed to live entirely on what I make, which is no small feat. I'm happy, Dad, really happy." She tried to force some cheerful enthusiasm into her voice, but unfortunately she didn't entirely succeed. How she wished she could brag about selling her articles. Surely she'd receive word of one soon!

"If you're so pleased about this change in jobs, then why do you sound upset?" her mother asked reasonably, joining the conversation from the extension line.

"I—I'm fine, really I am."

"Somehow, sweetie, that just doesn't ring true."

"I don't like the sounds of this," her father interrupted impatiently. "I made a mistake in arranging this Seattle assignment for you. It seems to me it'd be best if you quit whatever you're doing and move back to—"

"Dad, I refuse to quit now."

"I want you to move back home. As far as I can see, you've got one hell of a lot of explaining to do."

"It seems to me," Maryanne said after a moment of strained silence, "that we should both take time to cool down and think this over before one of us says or does something we're all going to regret."

"I'm calm." The voice that roared over the long-distance wires threatened to impair Maryanne's hearing.

"Daddy, I love you and Mom dearly, but I think it would be best if we both slept on this. I'm going to hang up now, not to be rude, but because I don't think this conversation is accomplishing anything. I'll call you first thing in the morning."

"Maryanne...Maryanne, don't you dare—"

She didn't allow him to finish, knowing it would do no good to reason with him when he was in this frame of mind. Her heart was heavy with regret as she gently replaced the receiver. Knowing her father would immediately call again, she unplugged the phone.

Now that her family had discovered she wasn't working at the *Review*, everything was sure to change. And not for the better. Her father would hound her until she was forced to tell him she'd taken a job as a waitress. Once he discovered that, he'd hit the roof.

Still thinking about what had happened, she put on her flannel pajamas and pulled out her bed. With the demanding physical schedule she kept, sleeping had never been a problem. Tonight, she missed the clatter of Kramer's typing. She'd grown accustomed to its comforting familiarity, in part because it was a sign of his presence. She often lay awake wondering how his mystery novel was developing. Some nights she even dreamed that he'd given her the manuscript to read, which to her represented the ultimate gesture of trust.

But Kramer wasn't at his typewriter this evening. He was giving a speech. Closing her eyes she imagined him standing before the large dinner crowd. How she would have enjoyed being in the audience! She knew beyond a doubt that his eyes would have sought her out . . .

Instead she was spending the night alone. She lay with her eyes wide open; every time she started to drift off, some small noise would jerk her into wakefulness. She finally had to admit that she was waiting to hear the sounds of Kramer's return.

Some time in the early morning hours, Maryanne did eventually fall asleep. She woke at six to the familiar sound of Kramer pounding on his typewriter.

She threw on her robe, thrust her feet into the fuzzy slippers and began pacing, her mind whirling at hurricane force.

When she could stand it no longer, she banged on the wall separating their two apartments.

"Your typing woke me up!" Which, of course, wasn't fair or even particularly true. But she'd spent a fretful night thinking about him, and that was excuse enough.

Her family had found out she'd quit her job and all hell was about to break loose. Time was running out on her and Kramer. If she was going to do something—and it was clear she'd have to be the one—then she'd need to do it soon.

"Just go back to bed," Kramer shouted.

"Not on your life, Kramer Adams!" Without questioning how wise it was to confront him now, Maryanne stormed out of her apartment dressed as she was, and beat hard on his door.

Kramer opened it almost immediately, still wearing the tuxedo from the night before, sans jacket and cummerbund. The sleeves of his shirt were rolled past his elbows and the top three buttons were open. His dishevelment and the shadows under his eyes suggested he hadn't been to bed.

"What now?" he demanded. "Is my breathing too loud?"

"We need to talk," she stated calmly as she marched into his apartment.

Kramer remained standing at the door. "Why don't you come in and make yourself at home?" he muttered.

"I already have." She sat on the edge of his sofa and waited until he turned to face her. "So?" she asked with cheerful derision. "How'd your hot date go?"

"Fine." He smiled grimly. "Just fine."

"Where'd you go for dinner? The Four Seasons? Fullers?" She named two of the best restaurants in town. "By the way, do I know Prudence?"

"No," he answered with sharp impatience.

"I didn't think so."

"Maryanne—"

"I don't suppose you have coffee made?"

"It's made." But he didn't offer her any. The fact that he was still standing by the door suggested he wanted her out of his home. But when it came to dealing with Kramer, Maryanne had long since learned to ignore the obvious.

"Thanks, I'll get myself a cup." She walked into the kitchen and found two clean mugs in the dishwasher. "You want one?"

"I have some," he said pointedly, stationing himself in the kitchen doorway. He heaved a long-suffering sigh. "Maryanne, I'm busy, so if you could get on with—"

"My father knows," she said calmly, watching him closely for some sort of reaction. If she'd been looking for evidence of concern or regret, he gave neither. The only emotion she was able to discern was a brief flicker of what she could only assume was relief. That wasn't encouraging. He appeared all too willing to get her out of his life.

"Well?" she probed. "Say something."

"What the hell have you been telling him?"

"Nothing about you, so don't worry. I did mention you to my mother, but you don't need to worry about that, either. She thinks you and I... Never mind."

"*What* does your father know?" Kramer demanded.

She sipped from the edge of the mug and shrugged. "He found out I wasn't on special assignment for the paper."

"Special assignment? What does that have to do with anything?"

"That's what I told my mother when I moved."

"Why the hell would you say something like that?"

"She was expecting me to mail her my columns, and call every other day. I couldn't continue to do either of those things. I had to come up with some excuse."

He cocked an eyebrow. "You might have tried the truth."

Maryanne nodded her agreement. If she'd bungled any part of this arrangement, it had been with her parents. Unfortunately there wasn't time for regrets now.

"Dad learned I moved out of The Seattle. I didn't tell him where I was living, but that won't deter him. Knowing Dad, he'll have all the facts by noon today. To put it mildly, he isn't pleased. He wants me to return to the East Coast."

"Are you going?" Kramer's question was casual, as though her response was of little concern to him.

"No."

"Why not?" The impatient look returned. "For the love of heaven, Annie, will you kindly listen to reason? You don't belong here. You've proved your point. If you're waiting for me to admit I was wrong about you, then fine, I'll admit it, and gladly. You've managed far better than I ever dreamed you would, but it's time to get on with your life. It's time to move back into the world where you belong."

"I can't do that now."

"Why the hell not?"

"Because... I've fallen—"

"Good Lord, Annie, it's barely seven and I've got to get to work," he said brusquely, cutting her off. "Shouldn't you be getting dressed? Walking around the hallway in your pajamas isn't wise—people might think something."

"Let them."

He rubbed his face wearily, shaking his head.

"Kramer," Maryanne said softly, her heart in her throat. "I know you didn't go out with anyone named Prudence. You made the whole thing up. This game of yours isn't going to work. It's too late. I'm . . . already in love with you.''

The whole world seemed to come to an abrupt halt. Maryanne hadn't intended to blurt out her feelings this way, but she didn't know how else to cut through the arguments and the denial.

For one wild-eyed moment Kramer didn't say anything. Then he raised his hand, as though fending off some kind of attack, and retreated from the kitchen.

''You can't be in love with me,'' he insisted, slowly sinking to the sofa, like a man in the final stages of exhaustion. ''I won't allow it.''

CHAPTER TEN

"UNFORTUNATELY IT'S TOO LATE," Maryanne told him again, no less calmly. "I'm already in love with you."

"Now just a minute," Kramer said, apparently regaining his composure. "You're a nice kid, and to be honest I've been impressed—"

"I am not a kid," she corrected with quiet authority, "and you know it. We both know it."

"Annie...Maryanne," he said, "listen to me. What you feel for me isn't love." His face revealed a bitterness she hadn't seen before. He walked toward her, gripped her shoulders and gazed down at her.

"That won't work, either," she said in the same quiet voice. She wasn't a poor little rich girl who'd only recently discovered who she was. Nor had she mistaken admiration for love. "I know what I feel."

She slipped her arms around his neck and stood on tiptoe, wanting to convince him of her sincerity with a kiss.

But before her mouth could meet his, Kramer abruptly jerked his head back, preventing the contact. He dropped his arms and none too gently pushed her away.

"Are you afraid to kiss me?"

"You're damn right I am," he said, burying his hands in his pockets as he hastily moved even farther away from her.

Maryanne smiled softly. "And with good reason. We both know what would happen if you did. You've done a good job of hiding your feelings, I'll grant you that much. I was nearly fooled."

"Naturally I'm flattered." His expression was darkening by the second. He stalked across the room, his shoulders hunched forward. He didn't say anything else, and Maryanne strongly suspected he was at a loss for words. Kramer was *never* at a loss for words. Words were his stock-in-trade.

But he was confronting emotions now, not words or concepts, and she knew him well enough to realize how uncomfortable that made him.

He'd hidden his feelings for her behind a mask of gruff annoyance, allowing her to believe she'd become a terrible nuisance in his life. He needed to disguise what he felt for her—to prevent her from learning what everyone else already knew.

Kramer was in love with her.

The mere thought thrilled her and gave her more courage than she'd ever possessed in her life.

"I fully expect you to be flattered," she said gently, "but I'm not telling you this to give your ego a boost. I honestly love you, and nothing my parents say is going to convince me to leave Seattle."

"Maryanne, please..."

He was prepared to push her away verbally, as he had so often. This time she wouldn't let him. This time she walked over to him, threw both arms around his waist and hugged him close.

He raised his hands to her shoulders, ready to ease her from him, but the moment they came to rest on her, he seemed to lose his purpose.

"This is ridiculous," she heard him mumble. He held himself rigid for a moment or two, then with a muttered curse buried his face in her hair. A ragged sigh tore through his body.

Experiencing a small sense of triumph, Maryanne pressed her ear to his chest and smiled contentedly when she heard his racing uneven heartbeat.

"You shouldn't let me hold you like this." His voice was low and hushed. "Tell me not to," he breathed as his lips moved through her hair and then lower to the pulse point behind her ear and the tender slope of her neck.

"I don't want you to stop..." She turned her head, begging him to touch and kiss her.

"Annie, please."

"I want to be in your arms more than anywhere. More than anything."

"You don't know what you're saying..."

She lifted her head enough for their eyes to meet. Placing her fingers on his lips, she lightly shook her head. "I'm a woman, a grown woman, and there's no question of my not knowing what I want."

His hands gently grazed her neck, as though he was still hesitant and unsure. Kissing her was what he wanted—she could read it clearly in his dark eyes—but he was holding himself back, his face contorted with indecision.

"Go ahead, kiss me," she urged softly, wanting him so much her whole body seemed to ache. "I dare you to."

His breathing was labored, and Maryanne could sense the forces raging within him. A fresh wave of tenderness filled her.

"You make it so hard to do what's right," he groaned.

"Loving each other is what's right."

"I'd like to believe that, but I can't." He lay his hand on her cheek and their eyes locked hungrily. He searched her face.

"I love you," she whispered, smiling up at him. She didn't want him to question her feelings. She'd say it a thousand times a day if that was what it took to convince him.

Flattening her hands against his hard chest, she leaned into his strength and offered him her mouth. Only moments earlier he'd pushed her away, but not now. His gaze gentled and he closed his eyes tightly. He was losing the battle.

It was while his eyes were closed that Maryanne claimed the advantage and kissed him. He moaned and seemed about to argue, but once their mouths met, the urgency took hold and Kramer was rendered speechless.

To her delight, he responded with the full-fledged hunger she'd witnessed in his eyes. He slid his hands through her hair, his fingers tangling with the thick auburn mass as he angled her head to one side. Maryanne felt herself savoring the taste of his kiss. It was so long since he'd held her like this, so long since he'd done anything but keep her at arm's length. She wanted to cherish these moments, delight in the rush of sensations.

So many thoughts crowded her mind. So many ideas. Plans for their future.

He tore his mouth from hers and nestled his face in the hollow of her neck as he drew in several deep breaths. Maryanne clung to him, hugging him as close as humanly possible.

"Kramer—"

"It isn't going to work—you and me together...it isn't right," he whispered.

"It's more right than anything I've ever known."

"Oh, Annie, the things you do to me."

She smiled gently. "You know what I think?" She didn't give him the opportunity to answer. "I love you and you love me and when two people feel that way about each other, they usually—" she paused and swallowed once "—get married."

"What?" Kramer exploded, leaping away from her as though he'd suffered an electrical shock.

"You heard me," she said.

"You're a crazy woman. You know that, don't you? A certifiable loony." Kramer backed away from her, eyes narrowed. He began pacing rapidly in one direction, then another.

"Marriage was just a suggestion," she said mildly. "I am serious, though, and if you're at all interested, we should move fast. Because once my father gets wind of it there'll be hell to pay."

"I have no intention of even considering the idea! In fact, I think it's time you left."

"Kramer, okay, I'm sorry. I shouldn't have mentioned marriage. I was just thinking, hoping actually, that it was something you wanted, too. There's no need to overreact." He had already ushered her across the living room toward the door. She tried to redirect his efforts, turning in his arms, but he wouldn't allow it.

"We need to talk about this," she insisted.

"Oh, no, you don't," he said, opening the door and steering her into the hallway. "Your idea of talking doesn't seem to coincide with mine. Before I figure out how it happens, you're in my arms and we're—"

"Maryanne!" Her father's voice came like a high-intensity foghorn from behind her.

Maryanne whirled around to discover both her parents standing in the hallway outside her apartment door. "Mom...Dad..." Frantic, she looked at Kramer, hoping he'd do the explaining part.

"Mr. and Mrs. Simpson," Kramer said formally, straightening. He removed his arms from around Maryanne, stepping forward and held out his hand to her father. "I'm Kramer Adams."

"How do you do?" Muriel Simpson said tightly as the two men exchanged brief handshakes. Her mother's troubled gaze moved from the men to Maryanne, surveying her attire with a single devastating look.

Until that moment, Maryanne had forgotten she was still in her pajamas. She closed her eyes and groaned.

"Samuel," Muriel Simpson said in a shocked voice. "Maryanne's coming out of...his apartment."

"It's not what it looks like," Maryanne rushed to explain. "Mom and Dad, please, you've got to listen to me. I didn't spend the night at Kramer's, honest. We just happened to get into a tiff this morning and instead of shouting through the walls and—"

"Samuel." Her mother reached for her father's sleeve, gripping it hard. "I feel faint."

Samuel Simpson clamped his arm about his wife's waist and with Kramer's assistance led her through Kramer's open apartment door. Maryanne hurried ahead of them to rearrange pillows on the sofa.

Crouched in front of her mother, Maryanne gently patted her hand. Muriel wasn't given to fainting spells;

clearly, she'd been worried sick about her daughter, which increased Maryanne's guilt a hundredfold.

"My little girl is safe, and that's all that matters," Muriel whispered.

"Listen here, young man," Maryanne's father said sternly to Kramer. "It seems you two have some explaining to do."

"Daddy, please." Jumping to her feet, Maryanne stood between her father and Kramer, loving them both so much and not knowing which one to confront first. She took a deep breath and blurted out, "I'm in love with Kramer."

"Sir, I realize the circumstances look bad, but I can assure you there's nothing between me and your daughter."

"What do you mean there's nothing between us?" Maryanne cried, furious with him. Good grief, she'd just finished spilling out her heart to the man. The least he could do was acknowledge what they shared, what they both felt. Well, if he wasn't so inclined, she was. "That's a bold-faced lie," she announced to her father, hearing Kramer groan behind her as she spoke.

Samuel Simpson, so tall and formidable, so distinguished and articulate, seemed to find himself at a loss for words. He slumped onto the sofa next to his wife and rested his face in both hands.

"Maryanne," Kramer said between gritted teeth. "Your parents appear to think the worst. Don't you agree it would be more appropriate to assure them that—"

"I don't care what they think. Well, I do, of course," she amended quickly, "but I'm more interested in settling matters between you and me."

Kramer's face tightened impatiently. "This is neither the time nor the place."

"I happen to think it is."

"Maryanne, please," her mother wailed, holding out one hand. "Your father and I have spent a long sleepless night flying across the country. We've been worried half to death about you."

"She didn't answer her phone," Samuel muttered in dire tones, his eyes narrowing suspiciously on the two of them. "If Maryanne had been at her apartment, the way she claims, then she would have picked up the receiver. We must have tried fifteen or twenty times to reach her. If she was home, why didn't she answer the phone?"

The question seemed to be directed at Kramer, but it was Maryanne who answered. "I unplugged it."

"Why would you do that?" Muriel inquired softly. "Surely you know we'd try to reach you. We're your parents. We love you!"

"That's it, young lady. You're moving back with us."

"You can't force me to leave Seattle. I refuse."

"This place..." Muriel was looking around as though the building was sure to be condemned any minute. "Why would you want to live here? Have you rejected everything we've given you?"

"The answer is obvious," her father bellowed. "She lives here to be close to *him.*"

"But why didn't her... friend move into her apartment building?"

"Isn't it obvious?" Samuel stood abruptly and stalked to the other side of the room. "Adams couldn't afford to live within a mile of The Seattle." He stopped short, then nodded apologetically at Kramer. "I didn't mean that in a derogatory way. You seem like a fine young man, but frankly..."

"I wouldn't care where Kramer lived," Maryanne informed them both, squaring her shoulders righteously. Any man she fell in love with didn't need to head a financial empire or be related to someone who did. "I'd live anywhere if it meant we could be together." Her eyes softened at her mother's shocked look.

"Don't you remember what it's like to be young and in love, Mom?" Maryanne asked her. "Remember all those things you told me about you and Dad? How you used to argue and everything? It's the same with Kramer and me. I'm crazy about him. He's so talented and—"

"That's enough," Kramer interrupted harshly. "If you're looking for someone to blame for Maryanne's living in this building and working at Mom's Place—"

"What's Mom's Place?"

"A very nice diner," Maryanne inserted quickly. "We do a brisk lunch trade and carry a limited dinner menu."

Her mother let out a small cry of dismay. "You're...you're working as a waitress?"

Miserable, Maryanne nodded. "But I'm doing lots of free-lance work. None of the feature articles I've written have sold yet, but it's too soon for that. I just found out the community newspaper's buying a couple of my shorter pieces, and I plan on selling them lots more."

"You might have warned me they didn't know about your being a waitress," Kramer muttered under his breath.

Samuel drew a hand across his eyes, as if that would erase the image of his daughter waiting on tables. "Why would you choose to quit the newspaper to work as a waitress?'' Asking the question seemed to cause him difficulty.

''It's honest work, Dad. I don't understand why you're acting like this. You're making it sound like I'm doing something that'll bring disgrace to the family name.''

''But your education is being wasted,'' her mother said, shaking her head. ''You could have any job in publishing you wanted.''

That much was true when it was her family doing the hiring, but when she was looking on her own, her employers were more interested in her job skills than who her father was.

''I'm afraid I'm the one who started this,'' Kramer interrupted. ''I wrote a column about Annie,'' he said bluntly. ''It was unfortunate, because I was out of line in some of the things I said, but—''

''Kramer didn't write anything that wasn't true,'' Maryanne hastened to say. ''He made me stop and think about certain aspects of my life, and I decided the time had come to prove I could make it on my own.''

''By denouncing your family!''

''I never did that, Dad.''

Samuel's shoulders sagged with defeat. The long hours her parents had spent traveling were telling on them both. They looked at her blankly, as though they couldn't quite believe even now what she'd been doing for the past month and a half.

''I did it for another reason, too.'' All three of them were staring at her as if they suspected she'd lost her mind. ''I'd met Kramer and we'd had dinner together and I discovered how much I liked him.'' She glanced at the man in question and saw him frown, knitting his brow as if he was looking for a way to stop her. "I'm sorry, Mom and Dad. I hated lying to you, but I couldn't see any way around it. I didn't want to worry you," she said, stepping next to Kramer and wrapping her arm around his waist. "I belong here with Kramer." There, she'd said it! "I won't be returning to New York with you."

"Maryanne, sweetie, you can't continue living like this!"

"I have a wonderful life."

Her father was pacing again. "You're in love with this man?"

"Yes, Daddy. I love him so much—enough to defy you for the first time in my life."

Her father's eyes slowly moved from his only daughter to Kramer. "What about you, young man? How do you feel about my daughter?"

Kramer was quiet for so long it was all Maryanne could do not to answer for him. Finally she couldn't stand it any longer and did exactly that. "He loves me. He may not want to admit it, but he does—lock, stock and barrel."

Her father continued to look at Kramer. "Is that true?"

"Unfortunately," he said, gently removing Maryanne's arm, "I don't return her feelings. You've raised a wonderful daughter—but I don't love her, not the way she deserves to be loved."

"Kramer!" His name escaped on a cry of outrage. "Don't lie. Not now, not to my family."

He gripped her by the shoulders, his face pale and expressionless. She searched his eyes, looking for something, anything to ease the terrible pain his words had inflicted.

"You're sweet and talented, and one day you'll make some man very proud—but it won't be me."

"Kramer, stop this right now. You love me. You're intimidated because of who my father is. But don't you understand that money doesn't mean anything to me?"

"It rarely does to those who already have it. Find yourself a nice rich husband and be happy."

She found his words insulting. If she hadn't been so desperate to straighten out this mess, she would have confronted him with it. "I won't be happy without you. I refuse to be happy."

His face was beginning to show signs of strain. "Yes, you will. Now, I suggest you do as your family wants and leave with them."

Every word felt like a kick in the stomach, each more vicious than the one before.

"You don't mean that."

"Damn it, Maryanne," he said coldly, "don't make this any more difficult than it already is. We don't belong together. We never have. I live in one world and you live in another. I've been telling you that from the first, but you wouldn't listen to me."

Maryanne was too stunned to answer. She stared up at him, hoping, praying, for some sign that he didn't mean what he was saying.

"Sweetie." Her mother tucked an arm around Maryanne's waist. "Please, come home with us. Your friend's right, you don't belong here."

"That's not true. I'm here now and I intend to stay."

"Maryanne, for the love of heaven, would you listen to your parents?" Kramer barked. "What do you intend to do once Mom's Place closes for remodeling?"

"Come home, sweetie," her mother pleaded.

Too numb to speak, Maryanne stared at Kramer. She wouldn't leave if he gave any indication he wanted her to stay. Anything. A flicker of his eye, a twitch of his hand, anything that would show her he didn't mean the things he'd said.

There was nothing. Nothing left for her. She couldn't go back to the newspaper, not now. Mom's Place was closing, but the real hardship, the real agony, came from the knowledge that Kramer didn't want her around. Kramer didn't love her.

She turned her back on him and walked to her own apartment. Her mother and father joined her there a few minutes later, obviously trying to hide their dismay at its bleakness.

"I won't need to give my notice," she told them, sorting through the stack of folded clothes for a fresh uniform. "But I'll stay until Mom's closes. I wouldn't want to leave them short-staffed."

"Yes, of course," her mother answered softly, then suggested, "If you like, I can stay with you here in Seattle."

Maryanne declined with a quick shake of her head, trying to conceal how badly Kramer's rejection had hurt. "I'll be fine." She paused, then turned to her family. "He really is a wonderful man. It's just that he's terribly afraid of falling in love—especially with someone like me. I have everything he doesn't—an education, wealth, and perhaps most importantly, parents who love me as much as you do."

MARYANNE HADN'T KNOWN it was possible for two weeks to drag by so slowly. But finally her last day of work arrived.

"The minute I set eyes on Kramer Adams again, I swear I'll give him a piece of my mind," Barbara declared, hands on her hips.

Kramer hadn't eaten at Mom's once in the past two weeks. That didn't surprise Maryanne; in fact, she would have been shocked if he had decided to show up.

"You be sure and write now, you hear? That Kramer Adams—he's got a lot to answer for," Barbara said, her eyes filling. "I'm gonna miss you, girl. Are you sure you have to leave?"

"I'm sure," Maryanne whispered, swallowing back her own tears.

"I suppose you're right. That's why I'm so furious with Kramer."

"It isn't all his fault." Maryanne hadn't told anyone the embarrassing details that had led to her leaving Seattle.

"Of course it is. He should stop you from going. I don't know what's got into that man, but I swear, for two cents I'd give him—"

"A piece of your mind," Maryanne finished for her.

They both laughed, and hugged each other one last time. Although they'd only worked together a short while, they'd become good friends. Maryanne would miss Barbara's down-to-earth philosophy and her reliable sense of humor.

When she arrived home, her apartment was dark and dismal. Cardboard boxes littered the floor. Her packing was finished, except for the bare essentials. She'd made arrangements with a shipping company to come for her things in the morning. Then she'd call a taxi to take her to Sea-Tac Airport in time to catch the noon flight for New York.

The next morning, dressed in jeans and a loose red sweatshirt, Maryanne was hauling boxes out of her living room and stacking them in the hallway when she heard Kramer's door open. She quickly moved back into her own apartment.

"What are you doing?" he demanded, following her in. He was wearing the ever present beige raincoat, his mood as sour as his look.

"Moving," she responded flippantly. "That was what I thought you wanted."

"Then leave the work to the movers."

"I'm fine, Kramer." Which was a lie. How could she possibly be fine when her heart was well and truly broken?

"I guess this is goodbye, then," he said, glancing around the room, looking everywhere but at her.

"Yes. I'll be gone before you're back this afternoon." She forced a trembling smile to her lips as she brushed the dust from her palms. "It's been a pleasure knowing you."

"You, too," he said softly.

"Some day I'll be able to tell my children I knew the famous Kramer Adams when he was a columnist for the *Seattle Sun*." But those children wouldn't be his...

"I wish you only the best." His eyes had dimmed slightly, but she was too angry to see any significance in that.

She didn't reply and the silence stretched, tense and awkward.

"So," she finally said, with a deep sigh, "you're really going to let me go."

"Yes." He spoke without hesitation, but she noticed that his mouth thinned, became taut.

"It may come as something of a surprise to learn you're not the only one with pride." She spoke as clearly and precisely as she could. "I'm going to do what you asked and leave Seattle. I'll walk away without looking back. Not once will I look back," she repeated, her throat constricting, making speech difficult. She waited a moment to compose herself. "Someday you'll regret this, Kramer. You'll think back to what happened and wish to hell you'd handled the situation differently. Don't you know it's not what you've done that will fill you with regret, but what you haven't done?"

"Annie—"

"No, let me finish. I've had this little talk planned for days and I'm going to deliver it. The least you can do is stand here and listen."

He closed his eyes and nodded.

"I've decided to haunt you."

"What?"

"That's right. You won't be able to go into a restaurant without believing you see me there. I'll be hiding behind every corner. I'll follow you down every street. And as for enjoying another bowl of chili, you can forget that, as well." By now her voice was trembling.

"I never meant to hurt you."

She abruptly turned away from him, brushing the tears from her cheeks with both hands.

"Be happy, Annie."

She would try. There was nothing else to do.

CHAPTER ELEVEN

"HAVE YOU HAD A CHANCE to look over those brochures?" Muriel asked Maryanne two weeks later. They were sitting at the breakfast table, savoring the last of their coffee.

"I was thinking I should find myself another job." It was either that or spend the remainder of her life poring over cookbooks. Some people traveled to cure a broken heart, some worked—but not Maryanne. She hadn't written a word since she'd left Seattle. Not one word.

She'd planned to send out new queries, start researching new articles for specialty magazines. Somehow, that hadn't happened. Instead, she'd been baking up a storm. Cookies for the local day-care center, cakes for the senior citizens' home, pies for the clergy. She figured she'd gone through enough flour in the past week to take care of the Midwest wheat crop. Since the holiday season was fast approaching, baking seemed the thing to do.

"But, sweetie, Europe this time of year is fabulous."

"I'm sorry, Mom, I don't mean to be ungrateful, but traveling just doesn't interest me right now."

Her mother's face softened with concern. "Apparently, baking does. Maryanne, you can't continue making cookies for the rest of your life."

"I know, I know. If I keep this up I'll look like the Goodyear blimp by Christmas."

Her mother laughed. "We both know that isn't true. If anything, you've been losing weight." She hesitated before adding, "And you've been so quiet."

When she was in pain, Maryanne always drew into herself, seeking what comfort she could in routine tasks. Such as baking. She was struggling to push every thought of Kramer from her mind. But as her mother said, she had to get out of the kitchen and rejoin the world. Soon she'd write again. Maybe there was a magazine for bakers—she could submit to that, she thought wryly. It would be a place to start, anyway, to regain her enthusiasm. Soon she'd find the strength to face her computer again. Even the sale of three articles hadn't cheered her. She'd stared at the checks and felt a vague sense of disappointment. If only they'd arrived before she left Seattle; then she might have considered staying.

"Is it still so painful?" Muriel asked unexpectedly. Kramer, and Maryanne's time in Seattle were subjects they'd all avoided, and Maryanne appreciated the opportunity to talk about him.

"I wish you and Dad had known him the way I did," she said wistfully. "He's such a contradiction. Rough and surly on the outside, but mellow and gentle on the inside."

"It sounds as though you're describing your father."

She pondered her mother's words. "Kramer is a lot like Daddy. Principled and proud. Independent to a fault. I didn't realize that in the beginning, only later." She laughed softly. "No man could ever make me angrier than Kramer." Nor could any man hope to com-

pete when it came to the feelings he evoked when he
kissed her. She came to life in his arms, like a wild-
flower blossoming in spring.

"He drove me crazy with how stubborn he could be.
At first all I could see was his defensiveness. He'd scowl
at me and grumble—he always seemed to be grumbling, as if he couldn't wait to get me out of his hair. He
used to look at me and insist I was nothing but trouble.
Then he'd do these incredibly considerate things." She
was thinking of the day she'd moved into the apartment and how he'd organized the neighborhood teens
to haul her boxes up four flights of stairs. How he'd
later brought her dinner. The morning he'd fixed her
radiator. Even the time he'd tried to find her a more
"suitable" date.

"There's another man for you, sweetie, someone
who'll love you as much as you love him."

A bittersweet smile crossed Maryanne's lips. That was
the irony of it all.

"Kramer does love me. I know it now, in my heart. I
believed him when he said he didn't, but he was lying.
It's just that he was in love with someone else a long
time ago and he was badly hurt," she said softly. "He's
afraid to leave himself open to that kind of pain again.
To complicate matters, I'm Samuel Simpson's daughter. If I weren't, he might have been able to let go of his
insecurities and make a commitment."

"He's the one who's losing out."

Maryanne realized her mother's words were meant to
comfort her, but they had the opposite effect. Kramer
wasn't the only one who'd lost. "I realize that and I
think in some sense he does, too, but it's not much
help."

Her mother was silent.

"You know, Mom," Maryanne said, surprising herself with a sudden streak of enthusiasm. "I may not feel up to flying off to Paris, but I think a shopping expedition at Macy's would do us both a world of good. We'll start at the top floor and work our way straight through to the basement."

THE TWO SPENT a glorious afternoon Christmas shopping. They arrived home at dinner time, exhausted, yet rejuvenated.

"Where was everyone after school?" Mark, the older of the Simpson boys, complained. At sixteen, he was already as tall as his father and his dark eyes shone brightly with the ardor of youth. "I had a rotten day."

"What happened?"

Every eye was on him. Mark sighed expressively. "There's this girl—"

"Susie Johnson. Mark's bonkers over her," fourteen-year-old Sean supplied, grinning shrewdly at his older brother.

Mark ignored him. "I've been trying to get Susie's attention for a long time. At first I thought she'd notice me because of my brains."

"What brains? Why would she do anything as dumb at that?"

Samuel tossed his son a threatening glare and Sean quickly returned to his meal.

"Some girls really go for that intelligent stuff. You, of course—" he looked down his nose at Sean "—wouldn't know that, on account of only being in junior high. Which is probably where you'll stay for the rest of your life."

Samuel frowned again.

"Go on," Maryanne urged Mark, not wanting the conversation to get sidetracked by her two brothers' trading insults.

"Unfortunately Susie didn't seem to be aware I was even in three of her classes, let alone that I was working my head off to impress her. So I tried out for the soccer team. I figured she'd have to notice me because she's a cheerleader."

"Your skills have been developing nicely," Samuel said, grinning proudly at his eldest son.

"Susie hasn't noticed."

"Don't be sure," Maryanne inserted.

"No, it's true." Mark signed melodramatically, as if the burden of his problem was too heavy to bear. "That was when I came up with the brilliant idea of paying someone—another girl, one I trust—to talk to Susie, ask her a few questions. I figured if I could find out what she really wants in life then I could go out of my way to—" he paused "—you know."

"What you were hoping was that she'd say she wanted to date a guy who drove a red Camaro so you could borrow your mother's to take to school for the next week or so." Samuel didn't succeed in disguising his smile as he reached for the salad.

"Well, you needn't worry," Mark muttered, rolling his eyes in disgust. "Do you know what Susie Johnson wants most in this world?"

"To travel?" his mother suggested.

Mark shook his head.

"To date the captain of the football team?" Maryanne tried.

Mark shook his head again.

"What then?" Sean demanded.

"She wants thin thighs."

Maryanne couldn't help it, she started to smile. Her eyes met her younger brother's, and the smile grew into a full-fledged laugh.

Soon they were all laughing.

The doorbell chimed and Maryanne's parents exchanged brief glances. "Bennett will get it," Samuel said before the boys could vault to their feet.

Within a couple of minutes, Bennett appeared. He whispered something to Maryanne's father, who excused himself and hurried out of the dining room.

Maryanne continued joking with her brothers until she heard raised voices coming from the front of the house. She paused as an unexpected chill shot down her spine. One of the voices sounded angry, even defensive. Nevertheless Maryanne had no difficulty recognizing whose it was.

Kramer.

Her heart did a slow drumroll. Without hesitating, she tossed down her napkin and ran to the front door.

Kramer was standing just inside the entryway, wearing his raincoat. Everything about him, the way he stood, the way he spoke and moved, portrayed his irritation.

Maryanne went weak at the sight of him. She noticed things she never had before. Small things that made her realize how much she loved him, how empty her life had become without him.

"I've already explained that," her father was saying. Samuel managed to control his legendary temper, but obviously with some difficulty.

Kramer's expression showed flagrant disbelief. He looked tired, Maryanne noted, as if he'd been working nights instead of sleeping. His face was gaunt, his eyes shadowed. "You don't honestly expect me to believe that, do you?"

"You're damn right I do," Maryanne's father returned.

"What's going on here?" she asked, stepping forward, her voice little more than a whisper. She was having trouble dealing with the reality that he was here, in New York, in her family's home. But from the look of things, this wasn't a social call.

"My newspaper column has been picked up nationally," Kramer explained, his gaze narrowing on her. "Doesn't that tell you something? Because it damn well should!"

Maryanne couldn't conceal how thrilled she was. "But, Kramer, that's wonderful. What could possibly be wrong with that? I thought it was a goal you'd set for yourself."

"Not for another several years."

"Then you must be so pleased."

"Not when it was arranged by your father."

Before Maryanne could whirl around to confront her father, he vehemently denied it.

"I tell you, son, I had nothing to do with it." Samuel's eyes briefly met Maryanne's and the honesty she saw there convinced her that her father was telling the truth. She'd just opened her mouth to comment when Kramer went on.

"I don't suppose you had anything to do with the sale of my novel, either," he demanded sarcastically.

Samuel Simpson shook his head. "For heaven's sake, man, I didn't even know you were writing one."

"Your novel sold?" Maryanne shrieked. "Oh, Kramer, I knew it would. The little bit I read was fabulous. Your idea was wonderful. I can't tell you how difficult it was to force myself to put it down and not read any more." She had to restrain the impulse to throw her arms around his neck and rejoice with him.

"For more money than I ever thought to see in my life," he added, his voice hard with challenge. Although he was speaking to Samuel, his eyes rested on Maryanne—eyes that revealed a need and joy he couldn't disguise.

"Oh, Kramer, I couldn't be more pleased." Her heart was so full it felt ready to burst.

"Do you honestly expect me to believe you had nothing to do with that?" Kramer asked again, more mildly this time.

"Yes," Samuel answered impatiently. "What possible reason would I have for furthering your career, young man?"

"Because of Maryanne, of course."

"What?" Maryanne couldn't believe what she was hearing. It was ridiculous. It made no sense.

"Your father's attempting to buy you a husband," Kramer growled. Then he turned to Samuel. "Frankly, that upsets me, because Maryanne doesn't need any help from you."

Her father's eyes were stern, and he seemed about to demand that Kramer leave his home.

Maryanne stepped directly in front of Kramer, her hands on her hips. "Trust me, Kramer, if my father was going to buy me a husband, it wouldn't be you! Dad had nothing to do with your success. Even if he did, what would it matter? You've already made it clear you don't want anything to do with me."

His only response was silence.

"I may have spoken a bit . . . hastily about not loving you," Kramer said hoarsely.

Samuel cleared his throat, murmuring something about giving the two of them time to talk matters out for themselves, and promptly left the room.

Maryanne stood gazing up at Kramer, her heart shining through her eyes. Kramer *did* love her; she'd known that for a long time. Only he didn't love her enough to discard the burden of his self-doubts. The boy from the wrong side of the tracks. The self-educated, self-made newsman who feared he'd never fit in with the very people who were awed by his talent.

"You were right," he grumbled, the way he always grumbled, as if she'd done something to displease him.

"About what?"

His smile was almost bitter. "About everything. I love you. Heaven knows I tried not to."

Maryanne closed her eyes, savoring the words she'd never expected to hear from him. Her heart was pounding so furiously that her head spun. Only...only he didn't say he loved her as though it pleased him.

"Is that such a terrible thing?" she asked. "To love me?"

"No...yes."

He seemed trapped by indecision, dragged down by their differences, yet buoyed by the need to see her again, hear the sound of her voice, gaze at her freckle-dotted nose and run his fingers through her hair. Kramer didn't have to say the words for Maryanne to realize what he was thinking.

"When everything started happening in my life, I thought—I assumed—your father was somehow involved."

"Did you really?" she asked, her words echoing with doubt. The excuse was all too convenient.

Kramer lowered his gaze. "No, I guess I didn't believe he really had anything to do with the sale of my book. Having my columns picked up nationally came as something of a surprise. For a while I tried to convince myself your family had to be behind that, but I knew it wasn't true. What really happened is exactly what you said would happen. You haunted me, Annie. Every time I turned around I could've sworn you were there. I've never missed anyone in my life the way I've missed you."

Her eyes misted. "That's the most beautiful thing you've ever said to me."

Kramer's look was sheepish. "I tried to tell myself your father was out to buy you a husband. Namely me. Think about it, Annie. He got you that job with the *Review,* and for all I knew, he could have made it his sole purpose in life to give you everything you want."

"I thought I'd proved otherwise," she said. "My parents went out of their way to make sure none of us was spoiled. I was hoping I'd convince you of that."

"You did." He slid his hands into the wide pockets of his raincoat. "I guess what I'm trying to say is that if your father was so willing to have me in the family, I'd be more than happy to take you off his hands."

"Willing to take me off his hands. How very kind of you," Maryanne snapped, crossing her arms in annoyance. She was looking for romance, declarations of love and words that came straight from his heart. Instead he was handing out insults.

"Don't get all bent out of shape," he said and the smile that stole across his lips was so devastating Maryanne's breath caught. "The way I figure it," he continued, "you need someone . . ."

Maryanne turned to walk away from him. Not any great distance, mind you, just far enough for him to know he wasn't getting anywhere with this argument.

"All right," he amended, catching her by the hand and urging her around to face him again. "I need someone."

"Someone?"

"You!" he concluded with a wide grin.

"You're improving. Go on."

"Nothing seemed right after you left. There was this giant hole inside me I couldn't seem to fill. Work didn't satisfy me any longer. Nothing did. Gloria and Eddie asked about you and I didn't know what to say. I was grateful Mom's Place was closed, because I couldn't have eaten there."

A part of her longed to hear all the romantic words a woman wants to hear from the man she loves. But it wasn't too likely she'd get them from Kramer. He wasn't telling her he'd heard her name whispered in the wind or seen it written in his heart. Kramer never would say things like that.

"You want me to move back to Seattle so I'll quit haunting you," she finally said.

"No. I want you to come back because I love you."

"And need me?"

He nodded. "I still think you could do a hell of a lot better than marrying an ornery old cuss like me. I promise to be a good husband—that is, if you're willing to put up with me . . ." He let the rest fade. His eyes grew humble as he slowly, uncertainly, pulled her into his arms. "Would you . . . be willing?"

She smiled, and hot tears gathered in the corners of her eyes. She nodded jerkily. "Yes. Oh, you idiot. I could slap you for putting us through all of this."

"Wouldn't a kiss do just as well?"

"I suppose, only..."

But the thought was left unspoken. His kiss was long and thorough and said all the tender words, the fanciful phrases she'd never hear.

It was enough.

More than enough to last her a lifetime.

Fall in love with

Harlequin Superromance®

Passionate.
Love that strikes like lightning. Drama that will touch your heart.

Provocative.
As new and exciting as today's headlines.

Poignant.
Stories of men and women like you. People who affirm the values of loving, caring and commitment in today's complex world.

At 300 pages, Superromance novels will give you even more hours of enjoyment.

Look for four new titles every month.

Harlequin Superromance
"Books that will make you laugh and cry."

PENNY JORDAN

Sins and infidelities...
Dreams and obsessions...
Shattering secrets
unfold in...

THE HIDDEN YEARS

SAGE — stunning, sensual and vibrant, she spent a lifetime distancing herself from a past too painful to confront... the mother who seemed to hold her at bay, the father who resented her and the heartache of unfulfilled love. To the world, Sage was independent and invulnerable— but it was a mask she cultivated to hide a desperation she herself couldn't quite understand... until an unforeseen turn of events drew her into the discovery of the hidden years, finally allowing Sage to open her heart to a passion denied for so long.

The Hidden Years—a compelling novel of truth and passion that will unlock the heart and soul of every woman.

AVAILABLE IN OCTOBER!
Watch for your opportunity to complete your Penny Jordan set.
POWER PLAY and SILVER will also be available in October.

**This October, Harlequin offers you a second
two-in-one collection of romances**

A SPECIAL
SOMETHING

THE FOREVER
INSTINCT

by the award-winning author,

Barbara Delinsky

Now, two of Barbara Delinsky's most loved books are
available together in this special edition that new and
longtime fans will want to add to their bookshelves.

Let Barbara Delinsky double your reading pleasure with
her memorable love stories, A SPECIAL SOMETHING and
THE FOREVER INSTINCT.

Available wherever Harlequin books are sold. TWO-D

HARLEQUIN
Romance

Coming Next Month

Available in October wherever paperback books are sold, or through Harlequin Reader Service:

In the U.S.
P.O. Box 1397
Buffalo, NY
14240-1397

In Canada
P.O. Box 603
Fort Erie, Ontario
L2A 5X3

"My Evening with the Debutante"

That unflattering article by Kramer Adams
started the whole thing. The "debutante" was
Maryanne Simpson, columnist at a rival Seattle
paper, which her father happened to own.

Despite her anger at Kramer's interfering
opinions, Maryanne decided the tough, streetwise
newsman was right about one thing: her life *had*
been too easy. She wanted to earn her own way.
And she wanted to earn Kramer's respect. No,
more than his respect . . .

She quit her job, left her luxury apartment and
gave up her trust fund—a Cinderella in reverse,
with Kramer Adams her reluctant prince.

HARLEQUIN

Romance

ISBN 0-373-03148-3